Verlie and Olive

A Novella

1.

Verlie Sue Martin was a purebred country girl. She helped birth pigs, and she skinned squirrels and rabbits three different ways. Two were conventional, but she didn't talk about the third. It involved a conjuring by Verlie that caused the animal to leap right out of its hide and die. She rarely used her third technique, and never on something other than hidebound game.

She was fifteen and petite, pretty with strawberry blonde hair and blue eyes and looked to be no more than eleven or twelve. Troy Cundliff told her it would be fun and would feel good. He was tall, slim and handsome, and she liked him. A big footed bastard, she called him when they bantered. Sometimes when they sat side-by-side on the creek bank fishing she'd put her little foot next to his and marvel at the disparity in size.

Anyway, Verlie told her best friend Olive Crowley it wasn't fun. It was nasty, and it hurt like hell. Maybe the other girls like it, but I don't, she told Olive.

Then Troy was gone. Someone started the rumor he left town and joined the Army, but no one knew for sure. No one in town ever saw Troy in the flesh again. Later, when things came to a head, all they found of Troy were his skivvies, his jeans with the cowboy belt buckled in the loops, and his plaid shirt still buttoned up to the neck. His work boots were laced up and tied with his socks stuffed inside.

2.

The Martins, the Crowleys and the Cundliffs all lived in the small town of Emery, Illinois, down near the southern tip of the state in the area they call Little Egypt. Since Emery was a small town, the members of the respective families knew each other, just like everyone in town knew each other. As the law of familiarity dictates, the complexities of their personalities were ignored. They really didn't know each other. They only knew what they saw or what they heard, the rumors, the assumptions and the ambiguities that dictate a person's reputation. They knew little of the real substance of their neighbors and didn't care to know.

The Martins—Frances and Little John and Verlie—lived on a small hog farm on the north edge of town. Their house was a traditional eight room farmhouse, small but serviceable. A gravel driveway led up to a concrete slab where a garage once stood that now was covered by a sheet metal canopy. This carport was used to house Frances's Chrysler 200 and Verlie's bicycle. Little John let his truck set out in the weather.

The house was surrounded by fifty acres of silty clay loam where Little John grew fair crops of corn and soybeans to augment his hog feed. About twenty yards behind the house was the hog operation comprising a sty, a clapboard feed house, a log smoke house and a well-ventilated farrowing house. There also were several squatty wooden A-frame shelters scattered about the sty to provide the animals refuge from the sun and rain. The farrowing house and the shelters were islands amid the fenced-in pigsty, the ground within the fence chronically worked up and muddy by the cloven hooves and ammonia-rich piss of a large herd of swine.

The Martins were austere and hardworking. They didn't socialize much, would speak when spoken to, and they occasionally attended the Pentecostal Church. What friends they had were church friends, but they weren't close to anyone. Little John smoked his Pall Malls outside the house and was known to sneak a drink on occasion but was never seen drunk. He was small in stature but was respected around town as being mean if trifled with, particularly in his younger days when he came home from the Army after serving in Vietnam.

Frances was younger than Little John, dour and unsmiling but efficient in the ways of a wife. She married Little John later in her husband's life when Little John decided he wanted to keep on living. They had only one child, Verlie Sue, who was born to their marriage in the first year. Verlie was lively and quick but thought odd by others ever since her baptism by water in the Pentecostal Church.

Verlie exhibited a selective precocity. She wasn't precocious in all aspects of her childhood. Just some. She had an advanced understanding of the ways of hogs. She also showed an advanced understanding of the tenets of the local Pentecostal Church. Frances, and sometimes Little John, started taking Verlie to Sunday services shortly after she was born. When she got old enough to be cognizant of the goings-on, Verlie thought the services were a great good time and, when she was still small, she'd dance around in the aisles when the brethren and sisters ran the aisles and sang gibberish. When she came home from church, she'd ape the preacher. It upset Frances.

"John, we need to stop that girl from acting the fool. It's sacrilegious."

"She's not hurting anything, Frances. Let her be."

"Hurting her immortal soul."

"I read Abe Lincoln did the same thing when he was a boy," replied Little John. "Mocked the local preacher to humor his friends."

"You know what happened to him," she said.

Although she chafed at the preacher's repeated pronouncements that women be subservient to men, Verlie shrugged it off, figuring she'd never be one to get married anyway and would never have a husband to kowtow to. Putting that irritation aside, she insisted on getting immersed and going to services every Sunday when she got older. It was her entertainment. When she was old enough, if neither Frances nor Little John wanted to take her, she'd ride her bike the five miles to the church.

Once inside the church the services started out like any other Protestant service, containing several sacred elements—Bible readings followed by hymns of praise. The preacher would deliver a robust sermon, working the brethren up to a fever pitch. Next would come the offering while the congregation was in a suitable giving frame of mind from the sermon. Sometimes the folks would partake of a spare Communion comprising grape juice and soda crackers.

Occasionally, but not every Sunday, Verlie was held spellbound when some of the brethren shouted their hallelujahs during the sermon and spoke their strange tongues and ran the aisles. On a really good Sunday, a fellow congregant might be led up to the front of the nave and one or two believers and the preacher would lay hands on the fellow, healing his ailments and cleansing his heart, causing the healed man to writhe with the delight at the return to sound health.

On Mondays, when Verlie went to school, she'd go through the entire performance for her friend Olive as they waited outside for the school bell to ring. Olive, being unchurched, begged her mother to take her to the Pentecostal Church, but her mother refused, once saying, "I got nothing against church, Olive. Maybe we should join a church, just not that one. I'm not sure it's a real church."

When Olive told Verlie about her mother's comments, Verlie spit on the ground and said, "It's the most real thing you'll ever see. I'm gonna get myself baptized in the Holy Spirit soon so I can work wonders and talk like them and run around the church. I'll show old Eva Crowley what for."

3.

Little John Martin raised hogs the same way his father, Big John, did before him. Frances raised vegetables to sell at the outside market in Emery on Saturday mornings and took in sewing. The folks in Emery thought they knew all there was to know about the Martins because Little John raised hogs and Frances was a truck farmer and seamstress. Since Verlie was an only child, Little John taught her everything about pigs that Big John had taught him. He told her if she learned the ways of the swine she'd never go without. To encourage her from a young age, Little John would give her a couple shoats out of each litter to raise and sell, the money being hers to keep or do with what she wanted. She kept her cash in a mayonnaise jar in a dresser drawer under her panties, confiding only in Olive that when she reached sixteen and had enough money, she'd buy herself a car and take off to see the whole country.

Sometimes Verlie helped in birthing the pigs, if help was needed, but she was rarely needed since most sows went about the business of having babies naturally. Her main task was to feed the shoats once they were separated from the sows and to feed the boar and sows morning and evening. It wasn't a hard job, but sometimes it could be risky, particularly if she had to get in the pen to free a little one that had its head lodged in a fence gap.

The sows were lazy and didn't present much of a threat to Verlie. Like a lot of mothers, once the babies were no longer sucking on their teats, they didn't pay them much mind and didn't view Verlie as any kind of a threat to their young. On the other hand, a boar could be dangerous. Little John had a prize Landrace boar he called Old Ott. Although Landraces were normally not mean, Old Ott had a streak, despite the fact he was fed well and allowed to mount the sows at will. Little John hoped the sows would farrow twice a year. He monitored their estrus and made sure they were available. He was an expert on when his sows were in standing heat, and he wanted to make Verlie an expert as well. Verlie didn't like that part of the hog operation. Sows in heat reminded her of her own cycles, and by fifteen, monitoring and maintaining her own periods was a gross inconvenience.

The Crowleys were relatively new to Emery. Rodney Crowley, a man of mediocre looks and middling intellect, moved to town about fifteen years earlier, married a local woman whom no one else was interested in, and bought a cheap, aluminum-sided, single level house in a necessitous area of town. Rodney was handy and remodeled the garage and tried to earn a few bucks as a scissors grinder and by repairing small engines. The businesses failed so he took a job on a section crew with the railroad. Being a gandy dancer was not a good job for a man considered a rounder. He'd be gone with his crew for weeks at a time, or just gone. Rodney Crowley was, from what others inferred, a dissolute drunk when off the job. But he did work. Olive, who was born shortly after they married, was their only child, although not for trying. Eva, Rodney's dutiful wife, suffered at least three miscarriages which some crones in Emery attributed to Rodney's brutish demands for satisfaction from his pregnant wife.

Their daughter Olive was plain, stout, and unhappy. She had bad skin and crooked teeth. Being plain and unclever, she didn't interest her father much and her mother worked long hours at Provinces Poultry Farms handling eggs, so Olive spent a lot of time alone and most of the domestic duties were left to her. Verlie was her only good friend and she longed to be petite and pretty like her. When she confessed that to Verlie one time, Verlie shrugged it off, telling her being attractive was both a blessing and a curse, and Olive should consider herself lucky being plain.

Anyway, the Cundliff parents, now both dead, had two children, Mae and Troy. The Cundliffs outwardly were the most prosperous of the three families. They had a brick ranch style home with a large garage building in the back on two acres just within the town limits. Tom Cundliff, tall and lanky, drove a semi over the road and made a nice living. He owned his own Peterbilt and kept it spotless. He drove mostly local routes and rarely did overnights. Elizabeth Cundliff, called Bess by her husband, cooked lunches at the local grade school. People in town thought the Cundliffs well off. The Cundliffs were active Methodists, not being well off enough, however, to join the Presbyterian Church. Still, money wasn't a problem and Tom never drove his Chevy pick-up truck for more than three years, and locals would pester the used car manager at Reister's Chevrolet for a chance to buy Tom Cundliff's trade-in every third March.

Mae was the Cundliffs' older child. She was tall and lanky like Tom, and not very pretty, like her mother. Mae married a man named Boone Tompkins from a nearby town right out of high school. They met at a dance at the Emery VFW Hall during the Christmas holiday of Mae's senior year of high school. Boone was the first boy to ever show any interest in the gangly Mae and she was smitten. Knowing Mae's prospects, her parents encouraged the union. After they married, Mae and Boone moved two towns over where Boone worked at the local grain mill. They had no kids of their own despite Boone's carnal persistence. Mae wanted a child, but it wasn't working out.

Boone and Mae were an interesting looking pair, with the angular Mae being a head taller than the thick-set Boone Tompkins. Most folks in Emery were gracious enough not to comment on Mae's bad luck in looks and some chuckled that if Mae and Boone ever had kids, the offspring would be better off favoring Boone, even if they were girls.

Troy, who disappeared, was two years younger than Mae, also tall and thin, but handsome in his own way; charismatic, some would add. He was a fair athlete in high school, playing baseball and basketball. He spent most of his spare time working at the Gas Mart, hunting and fishing, and driving his old Ford truck around Emery, often with a girl or two in the cab, sometimes with a load of boys in the bed. Troy wasn't a bastard at all, even though Verlie called him one, but an orphan after his folks died, which Verlie thought was a first cousin to a bastard, so no one bothered to look for him at first when he disappeared

Olive Crowley had her suspicions about Troy and what became of him. But she never said a word about it for a couple of reasons: Verlie was her best friend, and, over her fifteen years, Olive had gotten quite attached to her skin. Besides, Troy was a rotten boy of eighteen and whatever his fate, he'd earned it. Although Verlie and Olive weren't familiar with the concept of karma, it was each's opinion that most folks get what's coming to them sooner or later. Bad begets bad and it helped them make sense of life.

Verlie and Olive were sophomores at Emery High School. They had been friends since first grade. Olive was the only kid who'd sit near Verlie in class. Verlie didn't mind that no one else wanted to be around her. It was distracting to have anyone too near. If Verlie was within five feet of another, that person's thoughts flooded her mind, and it was distracting. Having Olive near her was no problem because there never was much going on inside Olive's head.

Despite her limitations, Olive was a decent student. She made up for lack of native intelligence by hard work and persistence. After the supper dishes were washed and put away, she'd lock herself in her bedroom and do her homework each night. She liked to study and read, which gave her respite from the housework and allowed her to avoid Rodney when he was home.

Verlie wasn't a great student based on her grades. She was plenty smart but distracted. Also, she didn't want to draw attention to herself by getting one hundreds on her tests by listening in on what her classmates were thinking, which she could do, so she intentionally messed up. She was concerned she'd be figured out. She about screwed it all up once when she was fishing with Troy. Verlie told him she could hear the catfish jabbering under a log down in Silver Creek. When he cast his treble hook with a glob of worms knitted on the barbs toward the log, the bait sank, and less than a minute later Troy had a hell of a bite, and it took him almost ten minutes to land a seven-pound flathead. Troy dismissed it as a lucky guess on her part, but Verlie was concerned Troy would put two and two together and suspect her of something. Fortunately, Troy was, like Olive, a dim bulb and the light never went on. Then he was gone.

4.

Olive got panicky when the sheriff's investigator came around asking questions about Troy Cundliff. Troy's big sister, Mae, although never particularly close to her brother, was trying to figure out why he joined the Army without giving anyone notice. If he did join the Army. Seems no one had any proof of that. Troy never mentioned the Army to his sister, who lived just two towns over and talked to him at least once every couple of weeks on the phone.

Mae had made a trip to the county seat to talk to the sheriff, Billy Phillips, about Troy. The sheriff knew Mae and her family. He originally was from Emery, and Mae and his daughter Jeanne had gone to school together before he was elected sheriff. Phillips had a soft spot for Mae. His shy daughter had few friends and Mae spent time with her and kept her from being miserably lonely. For her part, Mae thought the sheriff was a good guy, doting and solicitous around his quiet daughter. Mae believed him to be honest and a man she could trust.

"That's town business, Mae," Phillips explained to her from behind his desk. "Besides, Troy is over eighteen and can do what he wants".

"I don't want to tell him what to do, Sheriff. I want to know what he did do. You know how those town cops are," she said.

She tried to cajole Phillips into looking for her brother. She also tried giving him a sweet smile, but her homeliness detracted from the desired effect. The sheriff had been a town cop in Emery before being elected to county-wide office and knew the inner workings and deficiencies of the Emery police department better than most. He knew Mae was still upset over her parents' deaths, which she complained at the time weren't appropriately investigated. He also knew she was trying to jockey him into a position where he could show up the town cops, and despite of his reservations, his ego took the bait. To shut up Mae, and to burnish his own vanity, the Sheriff told her he'd send a sheriff's investigator to interview the town cops and talk to Troy's friends and try to get a lead on where he went.

The investigator, Detective Sergeant Sam Mank, a good-natured, laconic man, being reasonably bright nosed around Emery asked a few simple questions and soon uncovered the rumor that Troy had joined the Army. Whether he'd joined the Army was easy enough to track down, so Mank made inquiries through the local recruiter's office and the Recruiting Sergeant did some research and assured him there was no Troy Cundliff in the U.S Army, or any branch of the military for that matter, from around those parts, which piqued the investigator's curiosity.

Mank visited the local high school from which Troy had graduated the previous spring. It was a typical small town high school: one large brick classroom and office building, a Quonset-style gymnasium and a track. All the components were old, but well maintained. When he went inside, Mank found it quaint and welcoming. Nevertheless, although everyone remembered Troy, no one in the school office knew anything about Troy's current whereabouts. Mank made inquiries at the school about Troy's friends and the office secretary gave him a handful of names.

When he met with each of the boys on the list, he found most of them to be obtuse, not by design, but by nature. A couple of the boys, being boys, cracked wise about Troy's girlfriends. He had several, they told Mank. They made no direct averment that Troy messed around with young girls, but the gist was there. Mank got the impression they were nervous talking about Troy, that they considered him a tough guy who wouldn't take kindly to them talking about him if he wasn't gone from Emery for good. The detective didn't press the boys to identify the girls. He figured he could get that info when he needed it if word of Troy's whereabouts didn't pop up soon.

One name that kept popping up, though, through his various inquiries around town was that of Verlie Sue Martin. The high school secretary mentioned Troy and Verlie were friends of sorts and could be seen walking together in the school halls between classes when Troy was still in school. The secretary thought it unseemly that Troy, a senior, showed such interest in Verlie, then a freshman. Mank's further inquiries about

Verlie led him to Olive Crowley. However, instead of going directly to Verlie he started out by interviewing Olive. To get some background on Verlie, to freeze her in place, so to speak.

Olive Crowley was an anxious girl, with fingernails chewed down to the quick. Fact was, her friend Verlie always told her she was an aggravating worrywart during best of times, so she was a nervous wreck when she called Verlie to tell her about the investigator coming to see her.

"You don't know anything and there's nothing to know. You had nothing to say to him, Olive," Verlie told her. "Okay? Keep your mouth shut."

It wasn't a hint or a warning, it was a fact. Olive knew nothing about Troy or his disposition, although she had some suspicions. But Verlie had no idea what sort of rabbit shit might have rolled out of Olive's mouth if she got excited. Or tricked.

"I only told the cop that Troy and you were fishing buddies."

"True."

"He wanted to know where you fished."

"What'd you tell him?"

"The truth. I said you and Troy had a spot down on Silver Creek where you liked to go for catfish."

"That's true. You can never go wrong sticking to the truth, Olive."

Olive had told Mank a few more tidbits about Verlie and Troy, but she didn't tell Verlie what she told him. She knew she'd have to give Verlie wide berth for a while or Verlie would know. She couldn't help herself.

"Only thing you do know is that Troy left town."

"Right."

"You didn't mention the hurting part I told you about, did you?"

"No."

"Good girl."

Fact was, Olive immediately liked Mank and his easygoing manner and she would have told him anything had he asked the right questions. He was, like her, a slow talker, round in the belly. Not real attractive. He ingratiated himself to Olive by being earnest and engaging. He looked her directly in the eyes when he spoke to her, like she was a real person.

He smelled of Old Spice aftershave like her old man Rodney did when he was sober and cleaned up.

After talking to Olive, Mank went looking for the fishing hole. He entered the scrub that grew out to the roadside from the creek. He found the opening to a path leading from the side of the road, right at the spot Olive told him he could find a path leading to the creek. The dirt path was rough, crowded by maple saplings and wild honeysuckle. Underfoot were some narrow tire tracks, bicycle tires he surmised, since Olive told him the bicycle was Verlie's preferred mode of locomotion. He pushed his way through the undergrowth, wrestling with low limbs along the way. He barked his shin on the trunk of a broken off stink tree and snagged his trousers on a wild blackberry bush. Mosquitos swarmed around his nose and ears, causing him to swat and sneeze. Closer to the creek, tall cottonwood trees lined the bank. He stood under a cottonwood and looked down. The creek had high banks cradling fast moving water. It was called a creek, but Mank thought it looked more like a small, muddy river.

Mank saw a tramped down area of dried mud amid the cottonwood trees. There were footprints in the dirt; some long and narrow, some made by smaller feet. The longer, narrower prints were embedded deep in the dirt. Mank saw the prints were made by a work boot some time ago. They would have been eroded had they not been so deep in the creek mud. The smaller sneaker prints were made by another person, and they were fresher, positioned atop the boot prints. He saw they were made later than the boot prints; maybe days later, maybe later the same day, he couldn't tell.

There hadn't been any rain in Anderson County for weeks. He figured the boot prints were made right after the last rain. He could check out the date of the last rain easy enough. But he needed to get his hands on one of Troy Cundliff's boots to make sure he was on the right track, although he wasn't yet sure what good it would do him if he proved Troy was down at the creek awhile back. He wasn't there now.

Mank drove out to the Cundliff place. It was a neat brick home on a fair patch of land in a nice part of town. He saw a large pole barn type building out back. He got out of his car and looked around. There were no vehicles in the driveway. There was an accumulation of rolled newspapers, yellowed and damp, in the front yard and mail stuffed into the mailbox. No one had been around for a while. He considered taking the mail himself and looking through it for anything relevant. But he made a mental note to have the Sheriff tell Mae to drive by the house and pick up the mail and the papers and leave the mail at the sheriff's office for him to look through later. He didn't want to be accused of any kind of tampering.

The detective walked to the front porch and stopped again to look around. There were some muddy shoe prints that looked like sneaker prints on the concrete but nothing else of note. Mank tried the front door, but it was locked. He could have forced the door but thought better of it. If there was evidence inside, he didn't want to taint it. He made another mental note to see the magistrate to get a warrant to enter the Cundliff's house if it came to that.

He walked to the driveway and peered through a dirty window into the attached garage. The pane so grimy it was difficult to see through. He made out an accumulation of tools, a gas can, a lawn mower, some waders, fishing poles hanging on the wall, and a tackle box, but most notably an old Ford pickup truck he assumed was Troy's. The presence of the truck didn't alter one of his working theories: that the recruiter was wrong, and Troy really did join the military, maybe using a fake ID and an alias. He could have left his truck in the garage for safekeeping until he got back. But still, it was a major clue indicating Troy didn't pack up his truck and hit the road.

Mank walked around back to the outbuilding. He saw that it was a large garage, and he tried the utility door, but it was locked. He walked around to the side and peered through the window. Inside he saw a red Peterbilt tractor with a patina of dust. The garage also housed the accoutrements of a well-equipped truck garage: a large Snap-On tool cabinet, an air compressor, a work bench, shelves of motor oil and hydraulic fluid all aligned in an orderly faction. Nothing looked amiss, but Mank noted that if word of Troy didn't reach him soon, he'd have to go to the judge and get a warrant to search both garages as well as the house.

5.

Mank learned that, after he was orphaned at seventeen, Troy stayed living in the family home in Emery, although his recent visit to the house indicated Troy hadn't been there in a while. The county clerk's records showed the house was paid for and a release of lien had been recorded years ago. Troy had a job at the Gas Mart working nights and it was rumored that if underage drinkers wanted beer, they could get it from Troy. It was also rumored that on any given night, there'd be a covey young girls who'd snuck out of their houses hanging around the store for cigarettes and soda pop and to flirt with him. In any event, his job at the Gas Mart earned him enough money to pay the utilities and his sister pitched in on the taxes. Apparently, he bragged about having some cash in the bank from his folks' life insurance (which Mank verified was still there, adding to the mystery of his disappearance). He had adequate domestic skills, and he cooked and cleaned and did laundry, jobs that were his after his sister married and before his folks died, so he got by fine.

His sister Mae and her husband would drive over Emery every month or two, sometimes three, to make sure he made out alright. Troy's buddies told Mank the sister was an odd duck. Tall and lanky like Troy, but as homely as he was handsome. Somehow, she'd snagged a husband a few years back, not long before her folks passed, and she moved out of town. When Mank asked one of the boys if Troy had any enemies that he knew of, he told Mank that Mae's husband Boone didn't like Troy at all. When she'd visit her brother, her husband waited in Stanley's Tavern drinking and shooting pool. But the kid didn't consider Boone an enemy, so to speak.

Mank decided to go past Stanley's Tavern and ask a few questions. Stanley, the tavern owner, worked behind the bar washing glasses. Mank noticed Stanley was an old school bar man, dressed in a white shirt, black trousers, and wearing a tie. Mank showed him his badge and said he was looking into Troy Cundliff's disappearance. He needed information on Troy's brother-in-law, Boone Tompkins. Stanley stopped what he was doing and dried his hands on a towel. He told Mank he knew Boone well. Told him Boone drank beer and shot pool at his place whenever he was in Emery. When Mank pressed him as to whether Boone had ever said anything about Troy, Stanley recounted the one time Boone said anything at all about his brother-in-law:

"He's a stupid son-of-a-bitch," Boone had said to Mae when she came into the tavern to pick him up. "You know the word around town is he likes young girls," he added. "He's gonna get his nuts in a vice one of these days, Mae. Remember I told you so."

"That's the only time I remember Boone saying anything about Troy," the tavern owner told Mank. "It didn't bother me. I'd heard those rumors about Troy Cundliff for a while. I'd say it's true Boone didn't care for the kid. But other than that, Boone's a good old boy. Sometimes he drinks too much, but who wouldn't with a wife like Mae? But Boone wouldn't hurt a fly."

"What do you know about Troy's parents?" asked Mank.

"Nothing. Tom Cundliff wasn't a drinking man, and he never came in here. Only knew them from passing them on the sidewalk. Pleasant enough, I suppose."

Neither the boys nor Olive knew much about the older Cundliffs either. Olive told Mank that Verlie had told her Troy's folks were mean as sin and they forbade her from coming around to see Troy. Tom Cundliff told her she was just another little teenaged split-tail looking to get a belly full and she should skedaddle, or he'd sic the law on her. Seems Tom had also heard the rumors about his son and figured if they were true, the blame should be placed where it belonged—on the sluts like Verlie who wouldn't leave his boy alone.

Nevertheless, no one else Mank talked with seemed to think the Cundliffs were mean, but Verlie was tainted. Verlie told Olive that Tom Cundliffs' comments offended her. "I only went to Troy's house to see if he wanted to go fishing. Who did they think they were talking to? Some tramp?"

The more she thought about their effrontery, the angrier she got. She wanted to confront Troy about them but thought better of it. What could Troy do about it? He was as ignorant as they were.

"Fuck them Cundliffs all to hell," she said to Olive. "I'm done with the whole lot of them. They're bad people and like the preacher said in one of his raptures, 'an eísai kalá, tha zíseis gia pánta. Kai, an eísai kakós, tha petháneis ótan petháneis.'[1] I've never forgot that lesson."

---

[1] Greek: If you're good you live forever; if you're bad you die when you die.

6.

"I don't know much about what happened to the Cundliffs," Olive told Mank when he pressed her. "The town cop found them both dead in their truck along a back road leading out of town, naked as jaybirds, no signs of violence or anything else. Clothes in the bed of the truck, folded up neat and tidy. Weirdest thing that ever hit this town."

Olive had a quick spasm of regret that she told the investigator about the Cundliffs, but figured if he was worth his salt he'd find out anyway. That's when she realized her affinity for the man could be a problem if she didn't watch out.

Mank followed up on Olive's information. He visited the city police office in Emery. The Emery city hall was in an old stone building housing the mayor's office, the town police, and a two-cell jail. The police chief's office reeked of tobacco smoke. Fortunately, the chief was in, and after giving him his credentials and his reason for being there, Mank asked to see the Cundliff's official file. The chief was balky.

"Who cares what happened to Troy Cundliff?" he asked. "The Sheriff should be happy he's out of the county. I'm sure as hell glad he's out of my jurisdiction. Lot of mommas sleeping better at night knowing that boy's gone."

"His sister is hectoring the sheriff, and the sheriff told her I'd investigate it. He probably got some girl in a bad way and went on the lam. But if I'm going to do my job, I need to find out what happened to his folks."

Despite his reluctance, the chief left to fetch the file on the Cundliffs.

Mank stood in front of the chief's desk and looked around the office. It was stark and utilitarian. A few photos of the chief hung on the wall. One showed the chief being sworn in by the mayor. Another was a photo of the smiling chief decked out in his hunting clothes, down on one knee, a cigarette dangling from the corner of his mouth, holding up the head of a huge whitetail deer he'd shot, showing off the rack of antlers. There also was a picture of the chief accepting a certificate from a troop of Boy Scouts. All-in-all, the room itself was neat, clean and unimpressive. Just stale.

The chief's desk itself was a sight, however. There were papers stacked about in loose piles, a dirty coffee cup containing dark sludge sat near one edge, and a telephone with an array of buttons evidencing multiple lines, within arm's reach. An ashtray with a half dozen snuffed out butts, the source of the ashes scattered across the faux leather desk pad, was next to the phone.

"They were no prizes, either," the chief said when he came back and handed the file to Mank. "Thought they were better than other people. Anyway, don't leave the building with it."

The file was thin. Mank sat down on a bench in the vestibule and read through it twice. The coroner wrote the incident off to carbon monoxide poisoning. The coroner reasoned the couple pulled over to have a little fun in the truck and died. But Mank was perplexed. First, it didn't seem like the type of amorous behavior a couple married over twenty years would engage in. Still, with his experience, Mank knew to never take anything for granted, particularly folks' sexual predilections.

More troubling to him was that the first cop on the scene said the truck wasn't running. The key was in the ignition but turned off. Cundliff could have shut it down, he thought, but where did the carbon monoxide come from? No one, not the cop, not the coroner, not anyone, noted in writing that the Cundliffs were red. Bright red skin color is a principal sign of carbon monoxide poisoning. Was it an oversight, not writing it down? Was it so obvious to the coroner it went without noting, subsumed in his opinion of carbon monoxide asphyxiation? And the clothes. Who goes parking along a semi-busy road, takes off their clothes to diddle, folds them neatly and lays them in the bed of the truck?

Being an astute detective, Mank's first thought was whether there was a connection between Troy Cundliff's disappearance and his parents' death. But why wait two years to take off? What was his motive? There were a lot of other questions in Mank's mind when he handed the file back to the police chief. All he asked the chief was if he could talk to the officer and the coroner who investigated the deaths. The chief told him the cop was no longer on the force. He took a job in another state about a year ago. The coroner was dead. Mank had made a mental note of the cop's name and figured he could track him down if he needed to.

7.

Verlie caught a whiff of wood smoke as she rode her bike to school early in the morning. Although the days were warm, the nights had a chill, and someone had fired up his fireplace to take the chill out of the house. Verlie breathed in the vapor of the smoke, and she quickened her pedaling, stimulated by the familiar flavor that gathered on the back of her soft palate.

The smell and taste of wood smoke always excited Verlie. It recalled those early mornings when she and Little John got up before sunrise and went out in the cold and laid the fires for the kettle and the scalding barrel on butchering day. They were set up out by the smokehouse. Little John would pick a cold day to make sure no meat spoiled during the butchering. It usually was a Saturday, and Verlie was off school and butchering day was a picnic for her.

Little John would select two hogs around three hundred pounds each, one for his family and another to be split between two families from the church. He penned them in small holding crates. Once his friends arrived and the fires were hot, he picked up the first crate with the bucket loader on the front of his tractor. He'd drive the hog in the crate to the scalding barrel. He'd take his rifle, the old one Big John gave him when he was a boy, and place the muzzle between the hog's eyes and shoot it. He and his two friends would drag the dead hog out of the crate and fasten its back legs to a gambrel and hoist it off the ground with the tractor bucket. Once it was hanging from the gambrel, he'd put a pan under the hog's head and slit its throat, catching the blood for making blood sausage.

He'd once told Verlie that, in the old days, if it were really cold, one of the old timers might take a coffee cup and catch some of the warm blood and drink it, but Verlie had never seen a man drink a cup of blood, not even Big John when he still came around on butchering day. But there was something exotic about it and she told herself someday she'd try it.

Little John would test the water in the scalding barrel with a thermometer. He wanted the water to be at least 135 degrees but no more than 150 degrees, like Big John taught him. He lowered the hog into the barrel for a couple minutes and raised it back out. By that time, the hair was loose and easily removed with a bell scraper. Little John and his two friends would each take a bell scraper and scrape the hair off the pig's skin. The hair on the Landrace pigs was coarse but not thick, so scraping was an easy task.

Once the hog was scraped, it was ready for butchering in earnest. Little John would gut the hanging hog and let its guts flop into a bucket. The gutting process fascinated Verlie to the point her father had to keep telling her to get back or she'd get blood all over her clothes, but she'd still edge forward when his back was turned and try to watch every cut of the knife.

Little John had an old door placed between two sawhorses to make a butchering table. One of Verlie's jobs was to scrub the table with hot soapy water, rinse and swab it down with bleach, which she rinsed off one more time with clear water. Once the hog was properly scraped and gutted, it was plopped down on the table. Verlie found the next part of the process prosaic. It was cutting the carcass into hams and loins and bacon and chops and other parts. Nothing imaginative or fun. Sometimes she'd get bored and, when Big John was still alive, she'd wander over to where her father had situated him next to the kettle fire and watch the old man scrape the intestines clean for sausage casings. Later, the women would mix meat and scrap and run it through the sausage stuffer into the clean intestines to make pork sausage or blood sausage or liver sausage or what not. Verlie didn't care to make sausage; she thought it women's work.

The ritual of butchering was permeated by smoke. Smoke from the kettle fire, smoke from the scalding barrel fire, smoke from the butcherer's cigarettes. Verlie enjoyed those smoky mornings, enjoyed everything involved in the butchering and ever after the smell of smoke set her heart racing. Yet, one thing bothered her: she didn't like that the hogs had to be shot between the eyes with a rifle. She'd fed most of the hogs since they were shoats, and she accepted that being butchered for meat was the lot of a hog. Still, she reckoned there should be a better way to do them in.

Several years ago, on butchering day, Verlie stood by a crate containing one of the hogs waiting for the water temperature to rise in the scalding barrel. The wood smoke was dense and her eyes watered. The hog looked up at her with mournful eyes. Verlie believed she heard the poor hog pleading with her. As if the hog didn't want to die an ignominious death at the hand of a redneck farmer with a rifle. Verlie leaned against the crate and wished the poor animal would fall over dead. To her surprise, it did. The coarse hair on its hide loosened and fell off and gathered in a neat pile in the corner of the crate.

Little John attributed the animal's death to the stress of being penned too long in the small crate and paid little attention to the pile of bristles. But Verlie knew better. That's when she first recognized she had unusual gifts. From Jesus, she surmised. She didn't understand the gifts, but she understood, even as a preteen, that she'd have to be prudent with what she heard from man or beast and what she acted on. As she matured and learned more about her church, she looked back on her first experience as charismata.

After her experience with wishing the hog dead on butchering day, Verlie wanted to see if she could do it again. She knew she couldn't keep killing hogs that way; Little John would get suspicious. She started out with small animals.

Little John had taught Verlie how to hunt squirrels and rabbits. He taught her how to skin them for cooking. The game added variety to their meals, which mostly comprised various cuts of pork. When he thought she was old enough, he'd let her hunt alone. In the summer, early in the morning during squirrel season, it wasn't unusual to see Verlie headed to the small stand of oak, pecans, pignut and walnut trees that lined the back of their property, her twenty-gauge automatic shotgun resting on her shoulder.

The first time she went squirrel hunting after she discovered her gifts, she traipsed through the woods, keeping her eyes focused on the treetops. In a short time, she saw the leaves at the top of a pignut tree jostling. There was no wind, so Verlie figured there was a fat fox squirrel bouncing on a limb. Although her shotgun was loaded, she didn't take it off her shoulder. She focused on the shaking leaves and wished the squirrel dead, just as she had wished the hog dead on butchering day. To her satisfaction, the animal fell through the limbs and plopped dead near her feet. But to her surprise, the squirrel was skinned clean as a whistle with the falling hide caught on a low bough.

She knew she'd have to explain to Little John how she killed the animal since he reveled in his daughter's hunting skills and always wanted to know the details of her kills. She took the shotgun and fired it aimlessly into the air. She put the skinned animal in her game pouch and moved on to a large oak which had a pile of acorn cuttings around its trunk. Again, she spotted movement among the oak leaves, conjured the animal dead, and watched it fall, stripped of its hide, all the way down to the ground. She fired her gun in the air. After bagging two more squirrels, and firing two more shots at the sky, she headed back to the house to show Little John her bag of game. She knew he'd be proud of her. Outside of pork, squirrel was his favorite meat.

They'd raised chickens for meat at one time and gathered eggs, until Little John was out scattering chicken feed, and a peevish black rooster pecked him on the ass. Little John took umbrage, walked to the house and came out with his twelve-gauge and shot the rooster and all the fowl about the place and threw them into the hog pen for Old Ott and the sows to feast on. Verlie remembered the sound the bones crunching and the tenor of Little John's legendary ire when he said, "you won't be pecking anybody else on their ass, you black bastard," and walked back to the house to return the shotgun. Little John could be mean and decisive when aggravated.

8.

Verlie had thought a lot about how Troy hurt her and the more she thought about it, the angrier she got. She felt the pain. Not physical pain, but a pain in her soul, and it was getting more difficult to live with the discomfort.

That's what he really wanted from me all along, she thought. He didn't give two shits about me or my feelings. He pretended to be my friend. But if that's what he wanted, she would figure a way to use it against him.

Late one Friday evening just before Troy vanished, Verlie put on her jeans and a gray hoodie and stashed a hunting knife in its sheath in her hoodie pocket. She rode her bike to the Gas Mart, staying on the lighted streets to avoid getting hit by a car. When she coasted into the parking lot, Troy was easy to see through the front window towering over the cash register, sipping a fountain Coke, clad in a plaid cowboy shirt buttoned to his Adam's apple and faded Wrangler jeans. Verlie chuckled at his wide leather belt and gaudy belt buckle. Dumb bastard thinks he's a goddamned cowboy, she thought. Practices walking pigeon toed like John Wayne. Don't think he's ever rode a goddamned horse, she mused. Only young girls.

Troy looked towards the door and fashioned his practiced cockeyed grin when Verlie walked in.

"Hey, girl," he said. "What brings you in here tonight?" He leaned against the back counter, dipped one shoulder and hooked his thumbs in his belt.

"Been thinking," she said as she sidled up to the cash register.

"About?"

"About me and you."

"Really?" He stood up straight.

"To be up front with you, Troy, I don't think we gave it a proper try, you know?"

"I wondered when you'd come around to that," he said.

Verlie had half a mind to gut him like a hog right then and there, and she fingered the hunting knife inside her hoodie pocket. No, if Troy were found dead in the Gas Mart, the cops would write it off to a holdup or something, and that's not what Verlie wanted.

"I had to think about it a bit," she said.

"What do you think?"

"It wasn't so bad. I think I'd like to try it again."

"When?" he asked.

"What time do you get off tonight?"

"Eleven, like every night I work."

"Okay, here's the deal," she said quietly. "When you get off, drive out to our place and park out on the hard road about a quarter mile from the house. Walk through the side yard and around behind the feed house. I'll come out and meet you. You gotta be quiet, though. Don't want to spook the hogs and wake Mama or Little John."

Troy's eyes lit up. "I'll be there, babe. You can count on it."

Verlie rode her bicycle home in the dark. She went in the house and greeted her folks who were watching the nine PM news on television. She told them she was tired and going to bed early. She went to her room, closed the door and lay on her bed fully clothed for nearly two hours while keeping an eye on the clock setting on the dresser. She knew her folks were in bed sound asleep by ten thirty. She heard Little John's loud snoring. About quarter after eleven, she heard the hogs snuffling. She got up and looked out her bedroom window and saw Troy's lanky silhouette against the feed house door.

"Dumb bastard," she mumbled as she slipped out of her bedroom window. "Don't know front from back."

When she got up next to Troy, she took him by the hand and led him into the shadows behind the feed house. Troy reached down and squeezed her ass cheek. They were only about ten yards from the hog pen, and she heard the pigs. They were getting agitated. As was Troy. She didn't want to wake Little John, so she figured she'd best hurry. She closed her eyes and conjured. The next thing Troy knew, he stood totally naked in the middle of the hog lot. He was puzzled. He looked around but couldn't speak. He heard Old Ott grunting as the boar ambled toward him. He tried to shout but his mouth wouldn't work. He saw Verlie on the other side of the fence, and he tried to call to her to help him out of the hog pen before Old Ott lit on him, but he couldn't call out. Old Ott picked up his pace. Troy knew how mean the fat Landrace boar could be. He tried to run, but his legs wouldn't work. Just before Old Ott got to him, he reached down and covered his prick and nut sack with both hands, but Ott was quick. Troy saw him bare his teeth in the moonlight before he rammed him, mouth open, and took a chunk out of his hands and bit off his private parts. He wanted to scream but no sound came out. The last thing Verlie saw in the moonlight was Old Ott hunkering over Troy, ripping his flesh with his sharp canines and crunching his bones between his powerful jaws.

The lazy sows heard Old Ott chewing and they smelled the blood. Normally not aggressive, two of them trotted over to get a share. The sows started in on the fleshy parts of Troy's arms. Ott tried to intimidate them, but they wouldn't move. Just as well, Verlie thought, with that fat old boar and two sows feasting on him, there wouldn't be a scrap of Troy left by daylight.

Troy's clothes and boots were stacked neatly by the feed house door. Verlie picked them up and rifled through his jeans pockets and found his truck key and ten dollars. She carefully placed his socks in his boots and placed the clothes, including his briefs and tee shirt, along with the boots, in an empty feed sack. For weight, she dropped in a rusty single bit axe head Little John occasionally used as a door stop. She tied the sack closed with twine.

Early the next morning, before daylight and before her folks got up, she would drive Troy's truck to his house after going down to Silver Creek to sink the sack. That was her plan for the morning. But now, as she walked toward her house, she chuckled softly and over her shoulder toward what was left of Troy Cundliff in the sty, and *"Mihi vindicta, dicit Dominus"*[2] flowed out of her mouth, just the way she'd heard the preacher say it.

---

[2] Latin: "Vengeance is mine sayeth the Lord."

9.

The Sunday after Troy disappeared, Verlie rose early, showered, and dressed for church. When she came down from her room, her mother commented on how nice she looked and offered breakfast. Verlie knew she looked nice. She'd taken time to fix her hair and apply a little make-up, even though most women at her church didn't wear make-up. She'd cleaned and pruned her fingernails and put on her denim skirt and coordinated flower print blouse, with elbow length sleeves and buttoned cuffs. She looked forward to the day to be her day of vindication.

"After you finish your breakfast, I'll drive you to church," her mother said as she set a plate with two fried eggs and cured ham in front of her.

"You going, too?" Verlie asked as she buttered a piece of toast.

"No, I don't think I will. I have a lot of sewing to catch up on. People are going to start calling asking where their clothes are."

"You could, you know. Wouldn't hurt you. Where's Little John?"

"Out with the hogs. Where else?"

"I can ride my bike," Verlie offered.

"No, honey, not it that outfit. I'll drive you. When church is over, go to the church office and use the phone. Call me and I can pick you up."

"Why can't we have cell phones like everybody else?" asked Verlie.

"They're expensive," said her mother. "You know how Little John feels about those things. Devil's megaphone, he calls them. Use the church phone. The preacher won't mind."

Frances knew how long some of the services could last. It was unpredictable when it might end. "You eat plenty," she added. "It could be a while before you get home for lunch."

Riding in Frances's car, Verlie was excited. She wondered how to prepare herself for the service. She had no plans to repent or ask forgiveness. Not for what happened to that big footed bastard. But she thought the preacher would say something that would confirm her sense of righteousness in what she'd done. How would he know what to say? Jesus will tell him, she reckoned.

When she got to the church, members were already going inside. She started to get out of the car and Frances touched her hand. "Call when you want me to fetch you." Frances patted her hand, something she almost never did, and Verlie started getting her mother's thoughts and feelings about her, which embarrassed her and made her feel sad that she couldn't share her thoughts and feelings with her mother.

Once inside the church, she took a seat in a pew on the ladies' side of the nave. She studied the list of hymns numbers on the wall. She looked up the pages in the hymnal. The first song was *Mighty Army of the Young*. She was young but found no particular relevance to her situation. The first line of *Jesus Is Passing By* struck her as nearer the point: "Come contrite one and seek his grace, Jesus is passing by." Only problem was she didn't feel contrite. She quit looking for relevance in the morning's hymns. Maybe the preacher would have something to offer in his sermon to confirm she'd acted in the right way.

The service started with hymn singing. Although Verlie sang along, she felt no movement in her soul. She started to feel down. She looked around for support from the brethren, but why would any be forthcoming? She started to feel edgy and raw when the preacher picked up his Bible and took his position in front of the congregation. He held the book and shouted, "This is the infallible word of the Lord. Amen!"

"Amen!" echoed through the church by separate voices, sounding like one voice loud and strong, in unison.

"Today we're going to revisit the Prodigal Son, from Luke, chapter fifteen, verses eleven to thirty-two. I know most of you have your Bibles in hand, so turn to the Book of Luke."

The announcement by the preacher grabbed Verlie's attention. The Prodigal Son? What's that got to do with Troy and me? The Prodigal Son comes home to his father; Troy ain't coming home. His father is dead. What the hell? She felt her hopes deflate. She really believed the Holy Spirit was going to speak to her about her situation through the preacher. That's why she got up early. That's why she dressed herself up and came to church. Was she wrong? That never happened before. What happened to her intuition about such things?

Verlie sat through the sermon like a stone, hardened to the words. She wasn't inclined to holler. She didn't stand and wave. There was nothing in the sermon for her. She closed her ears and waited for it to end. All she could do was think about her actions regarding the Cundliff family and second guess herself.

No, she thought. I wasn't wrong. They were evil, the three of them. Fuck the Cundliffs all to hell, she thought. Not one of them was any good. Well, maybe Mae is, but the world's a better place with them other three gone. Lord have mercy, she thought. I did the world a favor. I saved a passel of those little girls from Troy. Now Jesus has turned his back on me.

Verlie phoned her mother from the church office. As she walked to the corner to wait for Frances, Verlie considered again the morning service and thought it a dud. She hadn't heard what she wanted to hear. There was little commotion, little entertainment. No one was healed. No one spoke in tongues. No one ran the aisles. She thought there'd be some hoopla. Some theatrics, some dramatics. But no. As to her actions *vis-à-vis* Troy, Jesus had left her hanging by ambiguities.

10.

Although unbeknownst to Mae, Detective Mank put in an admirable amount of time following up on Troy's whereabouts. These sorts of cases took time, but Mae was impatient. Boone, Mae's husband, tired of her constant haranguing, agreed to drive over to Emery on his day off and do some checking on his own. He'd rather have drunk beer and shot pool like he usually did on his day off, but Mae had a sharp tongue and pushy manner when she wanted her way, so he figured he'd make the effort and dull her edge a little. More importantly to him, and unbeknownst to Mae, Boone also wanted Troy accounted for so Mae could sell their parents' house, and he could pocket some of her cash.

Boone visited all the places in Emery where he thought an eighteen-year-old boy would go: the Gas Mart, where he'd worked, the pool hall, Ralph's Garage where the gearheads hung out, the movie house and the barber shop. No one had seen Troy in weeks. The clerk at the Gas Mart told him Troy stopped showing up for his shift without a word. He still had a paycheck to pick up. Boone began to think perhaps Troy had joined the Army and left town. But why would he leave money on the table? The law after his ass, maybe?

One oddity Boone discovered was that everywhere he went to ask about Troy, whoever he talked to told him a sheriff's detective already had been around. Boone wasn't plowing any new ground following the detective's harrow. He was frustrated, but at least he could tell Mae that Mank was doing his job, and she should give the detective a chance and that he himself had tried as best as he could, and she should ease up on him.

Before he left Emery, Boone thought he'd try one last thing. Boone was aware of Verlie Martin and her friendship with Troy. He thought better of visiting her, however. It wouldn't look good for a twenty-five-year-old married man to call on her, whatever the reason. Though small and quiet, Little John was an irascible son-of-bitch and Boone didn't want to deal with him. He drove past the Martin place and looked out of the open car window, the stink of pig shit nearly gagging him.

Something caught his eye. He saw Verlie rolling her bike off the carport. She jumped on it and headed down the driveway toward the hard road. Boone turned his car around and drove slowly back toward Verlie. He startled her when he pulled up alongside her and hollered, "Verlie!"

"What the hell, Boone," she said, trying to control the handlebar. "You almost caused me to wreck my bike."

Verlie stopped the bike and stood straddling the saddle. Boone stopped as well. They were parked along the road downwind from Little John's hog lot. The stench was eye-watering.

"What you want, Boone?" she asked.

"Mae's got me out looking for Troy. You know Mae."

"Not gonna find him around here, Boone. Haven't you heard? He up and joined the Army."

"Mae don't think he did."

"That's Mae's problem," said Verlie. "She mothered that boy too much, can't let him go."

"I got to live with her, Verlie. If he's not in the Army, I got to find him."

Verlie shrugged her shoulders. "Better you than me, Boone."

"If he didn't join the Army, I'll find him, Verlie. Mae will pester me til I do."

Verlie shrugged again.

"Or that detective will find him, one."

"Haven't met the man," she said.

"Damn, Verlie, how do you stand the stink out here?" asked Boone, waving is hand in front of his nose.

"Like Little John always says, 'it smells like money.'"

Verlie got on the bicycle seat and put one foot on a pedal and the other on the roadside.

"I got to get going, Boone. Give my regards to Mae."

"I will. If you hear anything out of Troy, let me know, okay, Verlie?" Boone asked as he drove off. "It would be a big favor if you help me get Mae off my back."

Verlie shrugged again as Boone drove away. She started pedaling, heading over to Olive's house.

Now I got that goddamned Boone snooping around, she thought as she picked up the pace.

"Fuck him all to hell, and I'm done with him, too," she said out loud as she pedaled faster, the breeze in her face carrying her words away. "He's a goddamned Cundliff by marriage and that's his bad luck."

11.

Olive was having trouble concentrating at school and her grades were slipping. At home, she had no appetite and couldn't sleep well at night. After she finished her homework, she would go to bed feeling tired, but sleep wouldn't come easily.

Even though Verlie often accused her of being empty headed, there were several matters of consequence running through her mind that kept her from concentrating at school, ruined her appetite and kept her awake at night. As an initial matter, she was on the edge of perplexity thinking about the Cundliffs. She couldn't help but wonder what really happened to Troy and his parents. It was all so strange. If something untoward was going on, why had Mae escaped the consequences? She was aware of Verlie's feelings towards the family. She knew Verlie had special powers and that worried her.

Verlie's powers also worried her because she could never be sure where she herself stood with her. She was her friend and had been for almost ten years. Yet recently, Verlie made a couple of veiled threats towards her. Nothing mean or spiteful, just enough to remind Olive who she was dealing with. It hurt Olive's feelings to think her friend had to try and keep her in line. What was that line? Thinking about Verlie soured her stomach, tainted the taste of her food.

Another thing that kept Olive awake was the thought of Troy hurting Verlie. She knew what Verlie meant when she said it hurt. She, herself, wasn't a child. Yet despite the threat of pain and discomfort, Olive couldn't help but wonder what it was like. What it might be like. Sometimes the thought excited her, got her blood up, and she'd touch herself.

More often, when a certain image entered her head, and her temples throbbed and her heart pounded, she imagined Detective Mank pressing against her in her bed. It didn't hurt. He was gentle and kind and smothered her with his soft flesh, the scent of Old Spice filling her room.

She didn't have that image often, but when she did, and she visualized her and Mank together until she was relieved, and she'd fall into a peaceful sleep that lasted until sunrise.

Once, however, she was awakened in the middle of the night by the scent of Old Spice. She opened her eyes to look for Mank, but he wasn't in the room. To her horror, Rodney loomed over her bed, showered and shaved and sober. She panicked.

"Get the hell out of my room!" she hollered, and Rodney receded into the darkness.

She lay in her bed until morning, not sleeping another wink, and when she got up for school, she couldn't decide whether Rodney had been in her room or if it had been a nightmare. Nevertheless, she started locking her bedroom door when she went to bed, and between her apprehensions about the Cundliffs and her prurient thoughts about Mank and her wariness of her father, she suffered intractable insomnia, lost her appetite and lost weight. She couldn't concentrate at school and started avoiding people, particularly Verlie.

12.

"Why you been avoiding me?" asked Verlie when Olive came out to the front porch of the Crowley's house. "You got something to hide?"

"Of course not," answered Olive. "I've been busy, you know, helping out my mom."

"Never bothered you before."

"You haven't been too friendly to me lately, either."

Verlie felt something from Olive. She looked around and didn't see Rodney's truck. "Your old man out on a bender, again?"

"Lord knows where he is."

"You don't have to live this way, Olive. There are ways to deal with a bad man."

"He's not so bad, Verlie. Just has a powerful taste for liquor. Sometimes when he's home and sober, he's okay."

"Sometimes shit smells like roast beef, but I still wouldn't want to eat any."

"What's that supposed to mean?"

"It means I think he's a nasty bastard," said Verlie

"That's my father you're talking about, Verlie."

"You disagree?"

Verlie turned her back on Olive and stood on the porch, arms akimbo, watching a young boy riding his bicycle down Olive's street. Nice style bike, she thought. Stingray type. She watched him until he turned onto a side street and rode out of sight.

Olive hadn't answered Verlie's question about her father. She shifted from one foot to the other, nervous in the silence Verlie imposed. She picked at a pimple on her chin, feeling awkward and ugly. She often felt that way around Verlie, whom Olive thought was pretty, having a sweet face, a clear and pale complexion, and a small body shaped just right, not fat or lumpy.

"Did you need something, Verlie?" Olive asked to relieve the tension.

"Wondered if that sheriff's detective had been around again," she said turning around to face Olive. "You haven't said much about him lately."

"I told him most everything I know," Olive said. "I figure he's done with me. Maybe done with the whole thing. Who knows?"

"I know his type don't give up easy if he's on a scent. No man does. I can't figure out why he hasn't come to see me? Everybody knows me and Troy fished and hunted together. You'd a thought I'd be the first person he'd come and see."

"That I can't tell you," said Olive.

"You sure you didn't tell him more than he asked for?"

"What do you mean?"

"I mean, did you tell him Troy tried to stick his pecker in me? You're the only person I told. Not even Frances or Little John."

"No, I never told him that." Olive flushed at the thought.

"It's like they say on those crime shows on television, Olive. A suspect needs means, motive and opportunity. He might see that as enough motive to make my life miserable. I don't need him harassing me."

"I never told him what Troy did to you."

"Good. Keep it that way. I don't need him breathing down my neck, too. I'm already concerned Boone's going to start pestering me. He drove by the farm this morning. Asked me if I knew where his brother-in-law was. Like I would know. That old scarecrow Mae put him up to it."

Olive felt the hostility in Verlie's voice. Normally, she didn't badmouth Mae, but Boone coming by the farm had set her off. Olive backed away from her a bit and stood closer to the front door. She tried to make her mind blank. Verlie squinted and stared at her. She didn't say anything, just stared. Olive turned red and started to sweat. She felt the pimples on her face throb.

"What you thinking about, Olive?" asked Verlie.

"Nothing, Verlie. I'm not thinking about anything."

"You never do, Olive. Your brain is what they call a 'tabula rasa'. That's why we're friends. Nothing going on in there," she said, tapping the side of her head with her index finger. "Anyway, if that detective does come around again, don't say anything to him about what Troy did.

Or about that son-of-a-bitch, Boone, either. I can deal with him if I have to."

13.

Mank decided he'd go back and interview a couple of the boys again. Although none of them came right out and said what they suspected, innuendo of Troy's proclivities was troubling. If Troy, as the boys implied, had a thing for young girls, it would not be out of the realm of possibility that someone's daddy, or mama for that matter, decided to take care of him in their own way.

At that point Mank decided to put Olive on the spot and ask her to come clean with him about the rumors and the boys' wisecracks. Olive might know more than she's saying. He felt Olive was well-meaning, but malleable. A good witness to get information from. He knew he could have gotten more information firsthand from Verlie, but he calculated her to be his trump card. Once he had more info, he'd interview Verlie and pin her down, see how she reacted to the allegations against Troy. That Troy abused her, or any other girl, was powerful motivation for someone to seek revenge against him, if revenge was a factor in his disappearance. Also, if the stories were true, Troy may have felt the local authorities were closing in on him, and he went on the lam.

Mank pulled into the driveway of the Crowley house. It was evening, near suppertime, and there was a vehicle in the driveway Mank assumed belonged to Olive's father. He jotted down the license plate number on his note pad.

As Mank walked up the sidewalk toward the front door he heard a racket coming from inside the house. It was a cacophony of curses made in a gruff man's voice, and squeals and crying from a girl. Mank rapped on the front door.

"Get the fuck outa here!" a man hollered. Mank listened closely and heard Olive whimper and sob. Mank banged on the door again, harder, but no one opened it.

"I said get outta here!"

Mank felt under his armpit for his service revolver. He put his shoulder into the door and pushed it open, stepping into the messy living room of the little frame house as Rodney was drawing back his fist.

"Don't you strike that child!" Mank shouted.

Rodney glared at Mank and took a step toward him with his fist still raised.

"Don't", said Mank. "Stay where you are."

"Who do you think you are, you son-of-a-bitch?" asked Rodney. "This ain't none of your business. It's family business."

Mank reached in his jacket pocket and took out a leather badge holder, flipped it open and held the brass detective's badge close to Crowley's nose.

"I could arrest you right now for child abuse," said Mank. He looked at Olive and saw a red splotch on her cheek and her hands were shaking. Olive stared at Mank with a solicitous look on her face that made him feel uncomfortable.

"It's okay, Detective Mank, he really didn't mean to hurt me," she said. "I provoked him."

"Why don't you and I go outside and talk and let him cool down," Mank said. He pointed at Rodney Crowley and said, "You've been warned."

When they were out on the porch, Mank asked Olive, "What was that all about?"

"He gets that way when he drinks. He came home and started in on me about the house being dirty and no food to eat. One thing led to another, and he accused me of running around too much, staying away from home."

"I see."

"But then he accused me of being one Troy Cundliff's girls. He asked me if I ever let Troy screw me. I couldn't believe he said that. I'm not like that, Detective Mank. I went off on him, slapped him across his nasty mouth. He lost it. Like I said, I provoked him, but what he said really upset me."

"I can understand that. But you shouldn't have hit him."

"I know. He made me so darn mad. I mean, I'm not like those other girls at all. Why would he ask me that? His own daughter?"

"Coincidentally, I came by to talk to you about that, Olive. I'd like to know the names of any of the girls Troy Cundliff was fooling around with. Do you know any?"

"Not for sure. Just rumors."

"Verlie Martin?

Olive paused.

"No, not Verlie for sure. Verlie's not like that either," she finally said.

Mank noticed Olive's reticence. "It's important you tell me the truth, Olive."

Olive rubbed a pimple on her chin, which still stung from Rodney's hard slap. She looked at Mank and wondered how badly Rodney would have beat her had the detective not shown up when he did. She shuddered as if chilled. But she felt a warm wave of gratitude and affection for Detective Mank break over her.

"He may have tried once," said Olive.

"Tried with Verlie Martin?

"Yeah, just tried. I don't think she liked it." She regretted what she had said as soon as the words were out of her mouth.

Just when Mank was about to ask her to elaborate on her comment, Rodney Crowley pulled open the front door.

"I want you out of here," he said to Mank. "I called the town cops and told them you're trespassing on my land. They told me if you don't leave, I should call them back and they'd come haul your fat ass to jail. They said they're tired of you sneaking around Emery poking your nose in shit that don't concern you."

Mank decided it wasn't the time to press Olive on Troy and Verlie. Or take on Rodney Crowley, who hovered in the doorway, his eyes bloodshot, a malevolent smirk on his face. Olive's hands shook again.

"I'm leaving now, Olive," Mank said, ignoring her father. "If you need anything, give me a call, you hear? Here's my card."

Olive took the card and impulsively grabbed Mank and hugged him, her face against his barrel chest, breathing in his spicy scent.

"I don't think you're fat," she whispered. "Don't pay any attention to what Rodney said."

Mank drove away from the Crowley home with plenty to think about. He was convinced solving Troy Cundliff's disappearance wasn't worth all the effort. From what he'd learned so far, Troy was a son-of-a-bitch and likely had a hundred reasons for leaving town. Nevertheless, he sensed Verlie Martin might be the key to unlocking the puzzle as to where Troy went. If he could get an answer for Mae and Sheriff Phillips, he could put this mess behind him and get back to his regular duties. His regular duties might bring him back to Emery someday, and it satisfied him to think about bashing Rodney Crowley in his goddamned drunken face if he ever found out he hit Olive again.

14.

Mae was perplexed that Mank hadn't yet talked to Verlie Martin. Everyone knew Troy and Verlie hung out together, hunting or fishing, sometimes riding around in Troy's pickup. Before Mae's folks died, Verlie would drop by to visit Troy, but their old man would run her off. Not everybody knew those stories. Mae thought Verlie was a deep well of information Mank hadn't bother to dip into. It didn't make sense to her he hadn't gone directly to Verlie. Mae didn't understand Mank's methods, so she drove out to Little John's hog farm after supper to speak to Verlie herself.

Mae saw Verlie's bicycle parked under the carport. She got out of her car and walked slowly up the driveway. Little John came out a side door and stood in the carport.

"Something I can do for you, Mae?" Little John asked, picking pork loin out of his teeth with a toothpick.

"Verlie home?"

"She's out back feeding the pigs."

"Can I talk to her?"

"If she'll talk to you."

Mae found Verlie in the feed house. Unbeknownst to her, Mae stood outside the feed house on the exact spot where Verlie had bagged up Troy's clothes and boots. The door was open, and Mae smelled the grainy, sweet dust from the hog feed. Corn, soybeans and sorghum. Verlie shoveled feed into a pail and didn't hear Mae knock on the wall.

"Verlie?"

Verlie spun around, startled by Mae's voice. "Dammit, Mae, why do you and your old man make a habit of sneaking up folks? Boone darn near caused me to wreck my bike a couple days ago." She looked hard at Mae and asked, "Little John know you're back here?"

"He told me I could talk to you."

"I don't have time to talk, Mae. I have chores."

"I won't keep you long. I want to find out what you know about Troy."

"I don't know any more about Troy than anyone else in this town knows, Mae," she said as she leaned her shovel against a corner post, wiped her hands on her jeans, and moved closer to Mae. She felt Mae's thoughts, and she didn't like what she felt.

"I need to know the last time you saw him, Verlie," said Mae. "And where."

"Let me think," said Verlie. She didn't like Mae's tone of voice. She was in no mood to be ordered about by a harpy.

She picked up the pail of hog feed and slowly edged her way out of the door past Mae. Old Ott smelled the hog feed in the pail and snuffled and grunted. He lumbered closer to the fence where Verlie dumped the feed in a trough.

"I don't remember the exact day, Mae," she said as she leaned on the fence and watched Old Ott gobble his food. "But it was a while back. I rode my bike out to the Gas Mart to talk to Troy about fishing. He said he didn't want to fish anymore, said he had more important things to do with his life than fish, and that was that."

Verlie felt the incertitude rising in Mae's mind.

"Did he say what those things were?"

"No, Mae. Troy didn't ever tell me much that was on his mind. Never anything personal. Other than he wanted to be a cowboy."

"A cowboy?"

"Yeah, the silly bastard told me a couple times he wanted to be a cowboy. Didn't you ever notice how he dressed or walked? He's your goddamned brother."

"Okay, so he wanted to be a cowboy. But did he ever say anything about the Army?" asked Mae.

"Maybe once. I don't recall, Mae. If he did say anything, I didn't pay close attention. Like when he said he wanted to be a cowboy. I'd a figured it was some more of Troy's bullshit."

Verlie felt the confusion set into Mae's head. She saw images of cowboys and soldiers swirling around in her mind. Hopefully she was good and confused. Confused to the point she wouldn't have to deal with her anymore. She didn't want to deal with her. Mae was okay.

Mostly homely and stupid, but she'd always been kind enough to her, even if her folks and Troy had not. But she didn't want to deal with her. She turned back to the hogs.

"You're my last hope, Verlie. Boone can't find his own ass with both hands and that detective is screwing around, wasting time."

"Have you prayed on it, Mae?" asked Verlie over her shoulder.

"You know us Cundliffs aren't the religious types, Verlie."

"You might want to give it a try. Miracles are real, Mae. Anyway, try praying over it. Works for me. Besides, I don't want to be anybody's last hope, Mae. Look at me. I'm a dumb kid." Verlie turned around to face Mae. "See?"

"Don't sell yourself short, Verlie. You got a lot going for you. You're cute, you're smart…"

"I don't know anything but hogs, Mae. I try to keep it that way. Keeps me out of trouble. I'm gonna be in trouble with Little John if I don't get these hogs fed." She turned away from Mae and proceeded to dump more feed in Ott's trough. "Look at the son-of-a-gun go after that hog feed, Mae. I swear. He'd eat anything you put in front of him."

Mae watched Old Ott root through the trough a minute or so then turned and walked away, her strides long and ungainly. Verlie glanced at her out of the corning of her eye and mumbled, "You're one lucky bastard, Boone Tompkins. One lucky bastard."

15.

Mae would give Boone no rest. "I'm convinced Verlie knows something about Troy; I feel it."

"You talked to her," Boone said. "What more can we do?"

"Go and talk to Frances or Little John. See what they know."

"I'm not going out to Little John's. He can be a prickly bastard. Besides, I don't think he knows about anything but hogs."

"Go see Olive Crowley. She's Verlie's best friend. See what she knows."

"Rodney's way worse than Little John."

"Go when Rodney's not there."

Boone knew he'd never get Mae off his back unless he talked to somebody. It was Saturday and he was off, so he got in his truck and drove over to Emery. Once in town, he stopped and got a beer and a hamburger at Stanley's Tavern. There were some loafers in Stanley's shooting pool. Boone put fifty cents on the pool table rail and said he'd play the winner. He had another beer and watched the game. When it was his turn, he ordered another beer and one for the boys who'd just played, picked out a cue stick that was reasonably straight, chalked the tip and said, "Challenger breaks."

Boone had a run of good luck. He won six games in a row and had a beer with each win. He was getting unsteady on his feet and decided if he was going to talk to Olive Crowley, he needed to do it before he got too drunk. On his way over to the Crowleys, he thought about what he was going to say if Rodney was home. But his good luck continued; Rodney's truck wasn't in the driveway.

Boone parked in Crowley's driveway. He saw Olive peek out the front window. He sat for a minute trying to figure out what to ask Olive. He wanted to frame it as Mae's inquiry, not his own. He didn't give a flying fuck about Troy, but Mae did. But he wouldn't say it like that. Olive was just a kid.

Boone got out of his truck and stood alongside it, hitching up his jeans and sweating. It was an unusually warm day, and his tee shirt stuck to his skin. He was sweating out the beer and he smelled himself, but he really didn't care. Olive was no goddamned prize, he told himself.

Olive watched Boone weave up the front yard to the porch. He knocked and she opened the front door and huddled behind the screen door. "What do you want, Boone?'

She stayed inside the doorway. She'd seen Boone stagger and smelled him and knew he had been drinking, and she was skittish around drinking men.

"Mae wants to know if you know anything about Troy," he said.

"No, Boone, I don't."

Boone eyed Olive from the porch. She hadn't gotten any cuter the last couple of years, he thought. He mentally compared her to Mae, who was tall and skinny, while Olive was short and thick. He saw her skin suffered. At least Mae had a decent complexion. He couldn't see Olive's legs or feet behind the screen door and imagined them to be unappetizing like the rest of her.

"I don't give a rat's ass about Troy myself," he finally said. "But Mae dotes on him and wants him home."

"Honestly, Boone," she said. "I never cared much for Troy either."

"What about Verlie?"

"What about Verlie?" she asked.

"Verlie ever say anything to you about Troy? Where he went or anything?"

"Verlie and Troy were just fishing buddies. I don't know that they talked about important things."

"I need to find Troy, Olive, or Mae will have my nuts."

Olive was used to men in Emery using foul language. It didn't bother her, although Boone's gesture of cupping his crotch when he said it was off-putting. Olive felt Boone's eyes on her and she knew anytime a guy was drunk like Boone, there was no way to predict what he might do.

"I don't know anything about Troy, Boone. I'd just as soon you leave before Rodney gets back."

"Where is Rodney?" he asked.

"Out."

"For how long?"

Olive didn't like the tenor of his question. Boone leaned forward toward the front door and braced himself against the jamb.

"He could be back any time."

"You one of Troy's girls, Olive?" Boone asked.

"Boone, you get your drunk ass out of here," Olive said, and pushed the front door closed.

"I don't know what Troy has that I don't have," hollered Boone as he started towards his car.

Olive was perplexed. Twice in the last few days someone asked her if she was one of Troy's girls. One of them was her own father and that cut still bled. Jeepers, I hate men, Olive thought as she watched Boone through the front window as he staggered to his truck. Fuck them all to hell, as Verlie might say.

16.

The next day at school, Olive cornered Verlie. "What the hell is going on? I had Boone Tompkins at my door yesterday wanting to know if I knew anything about Troy. Or if you did. The bastard was drunk and stinky. And rude. He wanted to know if I was one of Troy's girls."

"You?" Verlie laughed. "You? Really? I don't think Troy is very choosy, but you?" Verlie laughed again. "What'd you tell him?"

"I told him to leave before Rodney got home."

"You probably looked pretty good to him, Olive. He's been sticking his thing in that skinny old Mae these last couple of years. He probably wanted a girl with a little meat on her bones."

Olive was stung by Verlie's comment. She insulted her weight, for sure, but she also chafed at the underlying implication she might have let Boone have his way with her.

"I don't do that, Verlie."

"Oh, Olive. Lighten up. You on your period or something?"

"Maybe."

Verlie felt bad for Olive. Even homely girls like her get their period and odds are pretty good they'll never have a reason or a chance to make a baby.

"Did you say anything to Boone about Troy or me?"

"No."

"Good girl."

Verlie was close enough to Olive she could divine Olive told the truth.

"I don't know where this is going, Verlie, but that detective came around again. Now Boone."

"Not to mention Mae. She came to see me," said Verlie.

"What the hell is going on?" asked Olive. "What do you know about Troy?"

"As far as you're concerned, nothing. Everyone else ends up knowing whatever you know."

"I know I don't like Boone Tompkins, Verlie. He's a smelly creep."

"Boone is sticking his nose where it don't belong. I'm telling you; Mae is going to get that husband of hers in a bind one of these days." Verlie moved closer to Olive, causing her to back into her desk. "You smell funny, Olive. You been in your old man's Old Spice?"

Olive couldn't go anywhere with the desk behind her and Verlie in front of her. Her face turned scarlet, her acne throbbed, and she started to sweat.

"Never mind, Olive," Verlie finally said. "I don't give a good goddamn if you want to smell like a man."

It was time for class to begin. Olive, still red and warm, took her seat at her desk. Verlie sat behind her. She leaned over and whispered, "I don't think that asshole Boone Tompkins is going to bother you anymore. Trust me."

Verlie sat at her desk and closed her eyes tight. She heard their teacher droning in the background, but she ignored her. She concentrated until her eyeballs ached. She conjured up an image of Boone Tompkins. In her image, Boone was at the feed mill, climbing up a ladder on the side of a thirty-foot-tall grain bin to make a visual check of the residue in the inside. Verlie saw Boone's work boot on the rungs on the ladder, the right boot lace loose and dangling. Then she didn't see it.

Boone tripped over the lace on a rung near the top and fell over twenty feet, landing on the concrete pad under the bin, his head splitting open like a ripe mush melon. Verlie saw Boone's co-workers running towards him, stepping over the rivulets of blood flowing from his head and webbing out on the concrete. Boone's open eyes were fixed on the top of the bin, blank and unseeing. Verlie didn't need to see anymore. The blood made her queasy.

17.

Frances was at the kitchen stove frying bacon for breakfast when Verlie came in dressed for school. Little John sat at the table having his coffee, waiting for breakfast. Like every morning, he listened to the farm report on the local radio station, waiting for the livestock prices.

"Boone Tompkins is dead," Little John said to Verlie. "It was on the news."

"You're kidding me," she said. "What happened?"

"Sounds like he fell off a grain bin," said Little John. "Kilt him."

Verlie sat down at the table and poured herself a glass of milk. "Poor Boone,"

she said.

"Poor Mae," said Frances. "First her folks. Then Troy goes off somewheres and now Boone. Poor girl's had it bad."

"Some folks are cursed," said Little John. "Runs in families. No rhyme or reason. Bad breaks follow bad breaks."

Verlie had to squelch a smile. Bad breaks, all right. Old Boone's head broke like a glass balloon.

Verlie reached for a piece of toast and buttered it. She nibbled on the crust, trying to get the vision of Boone's broken body out of her head. She asked her mother for a cup of coffee.

"You don't usually take coffee," Francis said. "What's the occasion?"

"I'm tired this morning. I need a pick-me-up."

Her mother set a cup of black coffee in front of her. Little John passed the cream pitcher.

"Have some bacon before you go," said Little John. "I think this batch has the smoke right."

Verlie obliged him.

Arriving at school early, Verlie parked her bicycle in the bike rack and sat on the front step and waited for Olive to arrive. Olive rode the bus to school and Verlie watched as her bus pulled up in front of the high school. The door opened and after four or five kids exited, Olive clomped down the bus steps. Verlie waved her over.

"Boone's dead," Verlie said even before saying hello. "Little John heard it on the radio, on the morning news."

Olive was taken aback and couldn't say anything. Verlie sensed what she wanted to ask, so she answered. "The dumb bastard fell off a grain bin ladder and busted his noggin, I guess."

"When?"

"Yesterday morning, I suppose. Made the news this morning. I wonder if I should have Frances drive me over to Mae's house to express my sympathies. Mae was always good to me, the homely old thing."

"Jeez, Verlie, she lost her husband. Be nice."

"That don't make her better looking, Olive."

"What do you think she'll do now? She lost her mom and dad and her husband, and her brother took off. Somebody needs to find Troy and tell him about his brother-in-law."

"I don't think anybody will find Troy," said Verlie. "Mae couldn't find him. Boone couldn't find him. Your detective friend can't seem to find him, either."

"Maybe you could find him, Verlie."

"I don't want to find him, Olive," said Verlie as she headed toward the door. "Time for class."

18.

Rodney was home when Olive got home from school. He was sober. "Guess you heard about Boone Tompkins," he said.

"Verlie told me."

"Boone was another dumb bastard like Mae's brother. All he ever wanted to do is shoot pool and drink beer."

"You're not one to be talking about drinking," said Olive.

"Don't get lippy with me, young lady. I work hard as well as take my pleasures. You or your mother ever done without?"

"No."

"Then don't sass me. He was probably climbing that ladder drunk, if you ask me. Anyway, Mae should sue that mill if he weren't drunk. Somebody over there fucked up. Mae could get a good settlement."

Rodney was interrupted by a knock at the front door. When he opened the door, Detective Mank stood on his porch.

"I thought I told you to stay away from here," said Rodney.

"I talked to the town police chief. He told me I could talk to Olive whenever I needed to."

"Easy for him to say. It's not his home life being upset," said Rodney.

"This won't take long," said Mank. "I need to ask Olive a couple questions."

"I'm going to keep an eye on you through the front window. I don't want you messing around with my daughter."

Rodney Crowley has a nasty turn of mind, Mank thought as Olive pushed past her father and came out on the porch. If Rodney was as smart as he thought he was, he could have demanded to stay out on the porch and listen while Mank talked to Olive. She's a minor, after all. But being a blowhard, Rodney didn't think things through before he mouthed off.

Olive smiled at Mank; she felt good having him there. Mank waited for Rodney to close the front door before he asked, "Did you know Boone Tompkins?"

"I knew Boone a little. Not well. I know he's dead."

"You heard."

"Bad news travels fast, as they say."

"I heard he was going around town asking questions about Troy Cundliff," said Mank.

"Troy was his brother-in-law."

"Did he ever talk to you?"

"Yes."

"When?"

"Just the other day."

"What did he want to talk to you about?"

"He wanted to know if I had any idea what happened to Troy."

"Because you're Verlie's best friend?"

Olive felt the heat rising in her face.

"I don't know why. He said Mae was on his back about finding Troy."

"He thought you might know something?"

"I don't know what Boone thought."

"Did Boone have any thoughts on Troy's disappearance?

"None that he told me."

"How well did Verlie Martin know Boone?"

"Mae is Troy's sister and Boone was Mae's husband. Verlie and Troy were friends. She knew him that way."

Mank saw that Olive was getting agitated, nervous. He didn't want to make her uncomfortable, so he decided to change the subject.

"How has your father been treating you?" he asked with a tilt of his head toward the front window. "Any more problems?"

"No, he's been okay. He hasn't been drinking a lot lately. That's good."

"If he gets rough with you, let me know," Mank said, smiling at Olive.

Olive felt weak in her knees. All she could do was smile back at Mank and shake her head yes. Mank reached out and patted her shoulder. Olive thought she might faint as Mank walked toward his car.

Once in his automobile, Mank decided it was time to talk to Verlie Sue Martin. Verlie was, in Mank's opinion, the one person who knew Troy, her fishing buddy, the best. As well as his family, including Mae and Boone Tompkins. He had enough background. He had his suspicions; it was time for him to fish or cut bait.

19.

Detective Mank sat in the diner in downtown Emery sipping black coffee and going over his mental notes. There were only a few folks in the diner, but he felt their eyes on him. Word of his business in Emery had spread and he knew he was an object of curiosity and suspicion. He looked at his watch. It was almost three PM and school let out at three-thirty PM. His plan was to get out to the Martin's hog farm before Verlie got home and look around. He hoped to catch someone at home and ask a few questions, get what information her folks might have about her and Troy Cundliff. He left money on the table for the coffee and a tip and walked to the door. He felt the eyes following him out.

There were several things he wanted to clear up, not the least of which was what Troy and Verlie's actual relationship was. Were they only fishing buddies? If so, why would Troy have that sort of relationship with a fifteen-year-old girl? He needed to know for sure the last time Verlie saw Troy. Did he give any indication he was going to leave town? Did he ever talk about joining the military? Did he hint around about going on the lam? And why?

Mank wondered if anyone in Emery had a grudge against Troy. Were the rumors true that Troy had a thing for young girls? He knew he'd have to broach that subject gingerly, in the event Verlie had that sort of relationship with him. He needed to be careful raising the issue in front of her folks.

On the drive to the Martins, Mank concluded he was going to talk to the chief about taking him off this case. They had other cases he should work on. More serious cases. No one in Emery seemed to care what had happened to Troy Cundliff. Mank knew about Mae and her special relationship with the chief, but he'd about had enough. Now Boone was dead, and he reckoned Mae would get even more demanding and he didn't want the headaches.

It bothered him, however, to leave Olive Crowley hanging out to dry. He was concerned that once her father knew he wouldn't be coming back to Emery on a regular basis, Rodney Crowley might get rough with Olive. The black coffee roiled in his stomach when he thought about Olive cowering on the floor, hands trembling, fear in her eyes. But Olive wasn't his responsibility, he told himself. All he could do to assuage his concerns was to forewarn the Emery cops of Rodney Crowley's brutish tendencies and ask them to check up on Olive on occasion. Still, he felt badly about Olive.

Mank pulled into the Martin's drive. The carport was empty, but a pick-up truck was parked on the gravel. He looked in his rearview mirror and straightened his necktie and brushed back his hair. What the hell? He thought. What do I care what I look like? It's a goddamned hog farm, for Christ's sake, and about that time the stench from the sty seeped into his car. The odor caused him to cough and blink his eyes.

"I gotta get off this case," he said aloud as he crawled out of car. "Goddamned hogs. Goddamned flies."

Mank knocked on the front door but go no answer. He walked around to the back of the house and got a better view of the hog operation. He spotted a short, slight man in overalls and a *DEKALB* seed corn cap standing by an outbuilding. He had a plastic pail in his hand.

"Howdy," said Mank as he approached the man. He reached in jacket pocket and took out his badge. "Sam Mank. Detective sergeant from the county sheriff's office."

"I'm John Martin. Folks call me Little John. I heard you was in town," said Little John. "What you doing out here?"

"I'm trying to track down what happened to Troy Cundliff."

"Troy left town. Joined the Army is what I heard," said Little John, opening the door to the feed house. When he came out, Mank peeked inside the bucket. He saw a medicine vial and a plastic syringe.

"I haven't been able to verify that," Mank said to Little John as he shooed a pair of flies away from his face.

"What does this whole thing have to do with me?" asked Little John, turning around to face Mank.

"Did you know Troy?"

"Not very well."

"I was told your daughter, Verlie, was pretty good friends with Troy."

Little John fixed his eyes on Mank's eyes. "What'd you mean by that?"

"I didn't mean anything, other than I heard they were friends, fishing buddies or something, is what I heard."

"People in Emery talk too damn much," said Little John.

"I've found out most of them don't really have much useful to say," replied Mank.

For some reason that comment tickled Little John, and he laughed out loud. "Nothing useful at all is about right."

"I'd like to talk to Verlie, if you'll allow it."

"She's not home from school yet."

Mank looked around at the sty, the feed house and the smoke house. He saw the butchering kettle leaning against the smoke house wall and pointed at it.

"When I was a kid, my grandpa used to butcher a hog now and then. I liked to help," said Mank. "Although I wasn't much help."

"We still butcher once or twice a year," said Little John. "We eat a lot of pork."

"You've got a nice herd of pigs there, Mr. Martin."

"All Landrace. That's all we raise here. Same as my old man."

Mank looked at his watch. "Not to change the subject," said Mank. "But shouldn't Verlie be getting home soon?"

Little John looked at his wristwatch. "Could be. You never know about her. Sometimes she lollygags. She rides her bike to school. She might stop by the Gas Mart for a soda pop or ride over to Olive's house. But she's generally home in time to have some supper and help with the evening feed. It's a little odd she's late this afternoon, because I reminded her this morning we were going to worm pigs."

"Don't these flies about drive you nuts?" Mank asked as he swatted flies away from his face.

Little John answered with a snort, like he was blowing a maverick fly out of his nose. "Flies go along with it."

Mank grew impatient waiting for Verlie and making small talk with Little John. "I'm sure you're busy," he said. "You mind if I look around?

At your hog operation? My Grandpa raised those red hogs, Durocs, I believe. Yours have a different look about them."

"Help yourself," said Little John. "Like I said, they're Landrace hogs. White for the most part. Long in the back. Good bacon makers."

Mank stretched his neck to look into Little John's plastic bucket. "What's in the bucket, if I might ask?

"Ivermectin. I'm worming some sows. They're due to farrow in a couple weeks."

"I see," said Mank. "I'll look around and let you get back to your work."

"Don't get too close to that fat boar. Old Ott is vigilant and don't take kindly to strangers."

Mank watched Little John walk away before he started nosing around the smoke house and the feed house. Nothing caught his eye until he saw a footprint in the dirt behind the feed house. It was a long, narrow print, at least two inches longer than Little John's work boot. He got down on his hands and knees and studied the print up close. It was similar in width and length to the boot print on the bank of Silver Creek. He couldn't be sure when the print was made but he felt certain the two prints, this one and the one on the creek bank, were made by Troy Cundliff's boot, meaning Troy had been out to the Martin place sometime before he disappeared. Mank took out his cellphone and snapped a picture. He needed to talk to Verlie about the footprints. He'd waited about as long as he could tolerate the stink and flies, and when she didn't show up, he got in his car and left.

20.

Toward the end of the school day, Verlie got a feeling from Olive that the detective was going to come see her. She wasn't worried about him; she just didn't feel like dealing with him. After the last bell, she hurried out and got on her bike and went for a ride.

"Where would that goddamned detective go if he was looking for me?" she asked out loud as she pedaled away from the high school. "My house, I guess."

Verlie had a direct route to ride home from school. But that afternoon, she took a circuitous route through neighborhoods she rarely visited. The weather was mild, and the air was sweet, and she was in no hurry to get to the farm, with its pervasive odor of pig shit and wet dirt and Little John waiting for her to help worm the sows.

"That detective can go to hell," she said as she dropped some coins into the soda pop machine outside the Amoco Station. She'd decided not to ride by the Gas Mart, reasoning the detective may know enough about her and Troy to suspect she might go there. She also avoided Olive's house, although she really wanted to talk to Olive.

Verlie sat on her bike and took a big swig from her can of RC. The carbonation backed up on her and she belched loud and long. Olive was getting too tight with that cop, she thought. Poor, simple shit. Verlie sometimes felt Olive's feelings, and for a minute today at school, she was repelled by Olive's feelings for the detective. Old bastard, she thought. I may have to deal with him one of these days, particularly if he messes with Olive.

When she looked at her watch, she realized she'd wasted over an hour riding around Emery. She had one more stop she wanted to make, though. She took off pedaling as fast as was comfortable, heading towards the Cundliffs. When she arrived, she parked her bike behind the side garage where it couldn't be seen. She walked around the building looking in the dirty windows, satisfied Troy's truck was left just the way she parked it. When she saw the fishing poles leaning against the wall she had a pang of regret, even though in her mind, Troy got everything he deserved. But she missed fishing with the big footed bastard and rued the fact she had no one to hang around with down at the creek.

Driving away from the Martin place, Mank decided he would drive by the Cundliff house again. The footprint in the dirt behind the feed house intrigued him. He was determined to get inside the house and find one of Troy's shoes to compare to the print, and to the print down by Silver Creek. He could wait until tomorrow and have Mae drive over and let him in. But Mae was grieving the loss of her husband, and he didn't want to add to her misery by having her visit her dead parents' home. He would force his way in. Who was going to stop him? Troy wasn't around and the Cundliffs were dead. He would get inside and worry about the consequences later.

Mank parked in the driveway leading to the side garage. He noticed the mailbox was empty and the old newspapers gone. He got out and peeked in the dirty garage windows and everything appeared as it had the first time he looked. He went to the side door of the house and tried the doorknob, but the door was locked, as he assumed it would be. Mank put his shoulder against the door and pushed with his considerable bulk until the door snapped open. He stood inside the kitchen. He inspected the door lock and the jamb. There was no significant damage, so he closed the door and turned on the kitchen light.

The aura of the house was mid-century modern. The kitchen was neat and tidy, and he was impressed how clean and orderly it was, considering a teenaged boy had been living there alone for almost two years. The green Formica countertops were a bit dusty, but there were no dirty dishes in the sink, no food slopped on the counters, no spills on the oilcloth tablecloth. Dust had started to collect on the appliances and linoleum floor, but otherwise the room looked as if it had recently been organized and lived in.

Mank walked through the kitchen and into the living room. Again, he was impressed by the neatness of the place. There was a flower print sofa along the wall facing a wall mounted television, a large flat screen concession to modernity. A pair of matching side chairs with a brass floor lamp between them sat at right angle to the sofa. A magazine rack stuffed with old trucker magazines—OVERDRIVE, ROAD KING, TRUCKERS NEWS—sat on the floor next to the lamp base.

The living room had an arched opening into a hallway. Mank worked his way down the hall, glancing into a first bedroom, which was sparsely furnished and appeared unused. He walked into a small but serviceable bathroom on the opposite side of the hall and, at the end of the hall, a second bedroom across the hall from what appeared to be an unused master bedroom.

The second bedroom clearly was Troy's habitat. In the corner was a clothes tree with an assortment of tee shirts, blue jeans and hoodies hanging from the hooks. There was a desk covered with magazines. Mank picked up one and saw that it was tawdry pornography. He looked at the covers of the other magazines and saw obscene pictures of men having sex with young girls. The pictures made him sick to his stomach.

"Why am I wasting my time looking for this son-of-a-bitch?" he asked out loud, dropping the magazines on the desk in disgust. But the porn renewed his resolve to find the bastard before he could hurt another child.

Mank went to the closet and opened the door gingerly, wondering what other abominations he might find. It was a typical closet, however, with an array of clothing on hangers and a shoe rack on the floor. As he knelt on the floor inspecting the shoes, someone behind him asked, "Can I help you find something?"

Startled, he jumped up with a long narrow tennis shoe in his hand. He reached inside his jacket for his pistol with his other hand but stopped when saw a young girl standing in the bedroom doorway. She was small and pretty, with reddish hair, blue eyes and an impish smile. His gut told him it was Verlie Sue Martin.

"Who are you?" he asked.

"Verlie Martin," she answered. "Who are you?"

Verlie focused her eyes on Mank's eyes and didn't waver, an act he thought curious for a kid her age. He'd worked juvenile at one time and recollected most kids her age were reluctant to make eye contact with adults. Particularly adults with authority. Mank reached in his pocket the pulled out his badge. "I'm Detective Sergeant Sam Mank, from the county sheriff's office. I'm looking for Troy Cundliff."

"You won't find him here," she said. "He left town. Joined the Army."

"His sister doesn't believe that."

"Mae's an old hen," Verlie said. "She's upset 'cause her folks up and died. Then Troy lighted out for the Army. Now her husband, Boone, fell off a grain bin. Bad luck's been following Mae around; she can't understand it. But then, Mae never was too bright."

Verlie sidled over to the desk and picked up one of the porn magazines.

"You shouldn't look at that stuff," said Mank.

"This is where Troy gets his ideas," she said, dropping the magazine on the desk. "They say he's a real nasty boy. Good riddance to him, I say. Now the Army can deal with him."

"I thought you and Troy were friends," said Mank.

"We fished together, that's all," said Verlie. "I wouldn't say friends. He liked to fish, and I liked to fish."

"I've been wanting to talk to you," said Mank. "I'd like to ask you some questions about Troy."

"Not today," said Verlie. "I've got to get home. I've got to help my old man worm some pigs."

"I'd like to come by your place when you get home from school tomorrow. It won't take long. Your parents should be there when I talk to you, anyway."

"Little John will be there. He doesn't go anywhere. He's boring as dust."

Mank watched Verlie walk out of the bedroom as quietly as she'd walked in. He gathered up the porn magazines and one pair of Troy's shoes, a pair of Converse All-Star high-top tennis shoes, the closest thing to a boot he could find.

Mank had an odd feeling when he left the Cundliff place. He hadn't been prepared to meet Verlie Sue Martin. Something about her left him uneasy. She was a cute and soft-spoken little girl, but exuded an oddness Mank couldn't put his finger on. Even with his years of experience as a detective he couldn't read her. Yet, he felt she was able to read him, and she may not be forthright when he finally questioned her.

21.

Verlie cornered Olive at school the next morning. "I met your detective friend yesterday," she said.

"Did he come out to your place to talk to you?" asked Olive.

"According to Little John, he did. But I wasn't there. I'd stopped by the Cundliff's to check on the place. He was there, nosing around."

"No kidding," said Olive.

"You know I don't kid, Olive. I found him rummaging through Troy's closet, looking at his shoes. Why do you think he was looking at his shoes? I don't like it. He wants to come by the farm and talk to me after school today. I don't like that, either. If that goddamned Mae had accepted the fact that Troy went in the Army…"

"What do you mean?"

"Oh, never mind, Olive. Why do you have to be so goddamned slow on the uptake?"

"I don't follow what you're saying."

"I'm saying I'm tired of people asking me about Troy Cundliff. First it was Mae, then Boone, now the detective. Anyway, I guess I'll talk to him after school and tell him what I know, which isn't much. If that don't satisfy him, well, he can go to hell."

When Olive got home from school, she located Mank's business card and called his cell phone. She was relieved when he answered, "Mank here."

"This is Olive Crowley," she replied. "Can I talk to you?"

"Your father being rough on you again, Olive?" asked Mank.

"No, he's been pretty good since you talked to him. It's about Verlie Martin. She told me you're going to talk to her this afternoon."

"I'm on my way out there now."

"I wanted to tell you to be careful. Verlie's not like other people. Don't get too close to her. Give her space, okay? "

"What do you mean, Olive?"

"I mean, if you have things you don't want Verlie to know, keep your distance. You can talk to her and ask her questions and all that, but don't get too close to her."

"You mean physically?"

"Yeah, physically."

"That's a peculiar thing to say, Olive."

"Verlie's a peculiar girl, Detective Mank."

With that comment, which took all the nerve Olive could muster to utter, she hung up and Mank continued on his way to the Martin pig farm.

22.

Mank smelled the Martin place before he got there. He was about a quarter mile away enjoying the pleasant breeze through his open car window when the air carrying the odor from the pig sty hit him in the face. The stench worsened as he got closer, and he rolled up his window and wondered why anyone would want to live on a goddamned pig farm.

He saw Verlie's bicycle under the carport when he turned into the drive. He parked and walked up to take a closer look at the bike. The tire treads were not a unique pattern, but he didn't know anything about bicycle tire treads. He made a mental note of the tire brand and figured he could check out the bicycle tires another time if he had to.

No one answered the door when he knocked. He walked around back and out to the sty. He saw Little John and Verlie feeding the hogs. The stench of hog shit got stronger the closer he got to the pen. Verlie spotted him and waved.

"Mr. Martin," he said as he neared the pair. "Detective Sam Mank."

"I recall," said Little John. "The red pig man."

Mank chuckled. "Not me, really. My grandfather raised some Duroc hogs. That's as close as I come to being a red pig man."

Verlie was occupied dumping hog feed from a bucket into the feeder troughs. Little John didn't employ any of the new style closed feeders. He used old fashioned trough feeders that could serve as water troughs if necessary. Verlie, wearing a pair of rubber chore boots, edged along the fence and dumped ground feed into the troughs. The hogs crowded around, snuffling and grunting and pushing their way to the food, making a general racket.

"Be right with you," she shouted over her shoulder.

Mank took the opportunity to wander over to the feed house. He went behind the building to look at the footprints he saw the day before. Much to his chagrin, he found the prints obliterated by another set of prints. Mank reckoned this second set of prints would correspond to the gripping patterns on soles of Verlie's boots. He no longer saw how long or how wide the first set of prints were. "Goddamn it," he swore to aloud to himself. But he did have a picture on his phone.

When Verlie finished feeding, she took a bucket into the feed house and came out looking for Mank. She found him on the backside of the feed house looking at the ruined prints in the dirt. He motioned for Verlie to join him.

"Yesterday when I was here, there were clear footprints in the dirt right here. You got any idea how they got messed up?" Mank reached in his pocket for his cellphone to show her the picture he took yesterday but thought better of it.

"Didn't know they were here," said Verlie. "But those right there are mine."

She pointed to the deep grooves in the dirt.

"One of the shoats made a run for it last night. It ran toward the feed house, and I chased it around the building. Guess I ran right over this spot."

"You didn't realize you were stomping on a set of footprints?"

"Didn't look down."

Mank looked at the dirt. He didn't see any cloven prints. It didn't look to him as if a pig had run through the dirt. But he didn't say anything to Verlie and let it drop. He made a mental note about the lack of animal prints, however, in the event he later wanted to pin her down about smudging the footprints. He took out his cellphone and took a picture of the ground around the feed house.

Verlie giggled. "This is kind of silly. If you want a good picture, you can take one of the farrowing house, or Old Ott, or the pig shit."

Mank wasn't amused. He put his phone back in his pocket and abruptly asked, "Where is Troy Cundliff?"

"I guess wherever the Army put him," she said without a pause.

"What makes you so sure he's in the Army?"

"That's what I heard."

"From whom?"

"Just folks."

"The Army recruiter says he's not in the Army."

Verlie shrugged. "Don't know anything about that. I only know what I hear."

"Were you one of Troy's girlfriends?"

"No way!" Verlie retorted.

"Do you know any of his girlfriends?"

"Not really. Most of them are younger than me."

"I'd like you to make me a list of names of the younger girls Troy hung around with, okay? Maybe one of those girls or her family had something to do with Troy disappearing."

"I don't think he disappeared. I think he wanted folks to think he disappeared. If I had to guess, I'd say he parked his truck in the garage, packed a bag and took off. Could be some girl's daddy was hot on his heels; could be he wanted to be a soldier. Or a cowboy. I don't know. He never told me he was leaving."

Verlie moved closer to Mank. She smelled his spicy cologne and saw the stubble of his afternoon whiskers. He smelled like Olive. She was standing next to Mank when Little John walked up, eavesdropping. Mank recalled Olive's warning and stepped away from Verlie.

"Don't know why you're wasting all this time and taxpayer money on that son-of-a-bitch Troy Cundliff. I say good riddance to bad rubbish," Little John said to Mank

Mank didn't respond. He made a mental note that Little John Martin didn't like Troy Cundliff at all. So far, he hadn't found anyone who was sorry Troy Cundliff was gone, except perhaps his sister Mae. With her husband dead, she was going to be fixated on finding her brother. Mank again entertained the thought that it was time to withdraw from the investigation and let Sheriff Phillips handle it.

He also second-guessed himself. Maybe he was wrong waiting to interview Verlie Sue Martin. It gave her a lot of time to get a story together. If he'd have gotten to her earlier, she may not have had time to cover up the footprints. She was a clever young girl, and he wasn't going to be able to trick her into divulging any useful information, if she had any.

"It's about suppertime, Verlie," said Little John.

"I thought you feed the pigs after supper," said Mank.

"I knew you were coming out, so I started early," Verlie responded. "Pigs'll eat anytime you give 'em something."

"I have a couple of things to clear up," said Mank. "You and Troy were fishing buddies, right?"

"Right," answered Verlie.

"Anyone else ever fish with you?"

"No."

"Did you fish anywhere but Silver Creek?"

"No, that was our spot. We always went there. That's the only place I ever went with Troy."

Something about her answer intrigued Mank. That place, thought Mank. There's something about that place.

"I'm going up to the house," said Little John. "Verlie, you come along shortly."

Mank said, "We're about done here, anyway. Go on and have your supper. Work on that list for me tonight, alright?"

'That place; that place' echoed through Mank's mind as he walked away. The thought of it made him itch. But he felt there was something special about that place where Verlie Sue and Troy often fished. Perhaps he needed to go back out to Silver Creek and do some more digging around.

After supper, when the dishes were done and Frances was sewing and Little John had fallen asleep in his recliner, Verlie announced she was going to her room to do homework. She carried the extension phone into her room and dialed Olive's number.

"Verlie?" Olive answered.

"Yeah, it's me."

"What's going on? What's the matter?"

"Nothing's the matter. Can't I call a friend on the phone? Does something always have to be the matter?"

Olive started to get nervous due to the tone of Verlie's voice. "You almost never call me, Verlie. It's odd."

"I'm odd, Olive. Anyway, I wanted to let you know your cop friend was out here this afternoon. "

"And?"

"I don't like him. He's a nosey bastard. You know what?"

"What?"

"I don't care if you like him or not. Fuck him all to hell, Olive. I'm done with him."

Olive was struck with panic when she hung up the phone. She'd heard Verlie swear like that before and it always ended badly. She didn't know what to do.

That night, Olive couldn't sleep. She tossed and turned and thought about Detective Mank and the ramifications of Verlie's comments. She didn't want him to come to any harm if she could prevent it. She couldn't decide whether she should call Mank or not. He might think her looney for taking Verlie seriously. Moreover, Verlie might take offense at her intrusion, and then what? It was a hell of a predicament, and she lay in bed all night staring at the ceiling, rolling it around in her head, to no avail.

23.

After talking to Verlie Martin, Detective Mank reported back to Sheriff Phillips. He explained he was making very little headway in the matter and was anxious to give it up.

"You're giving up? You can't do that, Sam. What am I supposed to tell Mae Tompkins? I owe her, Sam."

He snubbed out his cigarette and looked up at the detective.

"Look, Billy," said Mank. "No one in Emery gives a good goddamn about Troy Cundliff. No one knows anything about his whereabouts. Tell Mae all I learned about her brother is that he's a goddamned pedophile and no one likes him."

"You know I can't do that." Sheriff Phillips had an anxious look on his face. "You have no more leads?"

"Just a hunch. And it's just a hunch, mind you. I think his disappearance might have something to do with his fishing hole down on Silver Creek. He spent a lot of time there, particularly with the Martin girl."

"Can't you go back out there and look around? Maybe there's something you missed?"

"I do have an idea along those lines," said Mank. "But I need your cooperation."

"Okay, Sam, out with it. What do you want from me?"

"I need you to authorize an underwater search. I'd like to get the fire department divers out there to look around in the creek."

Billy Phillips lit another cigarette and blew the smoke towards the ceiling. He sat in his chair and stared across the desk at Mank.

"Well played, Sam," he finally said, smoke rolling out of his nostrils. "Well played. You come in here and threaten to quit the case and then ask the department to spend money on divers. Where does that put me?"

Mank smiled. It put Sheriff Phillips right where he wanted him.

"This is the last thing, Billy," said Mank. "If a search of the creek doesn't produce anything, then we pull the plug and you'll have to tell Mae Tompkins we've reached a dead end."

24.

Olive wasn't great at math, but she wasn't stupid either. She started adding things up and the number of coincidences startled her. She decided to take her thoughts to Mank before Verlie could hurt him.

Olive called the detective to tell him everything she knew. For example, she explained to him that Troy's parents warned Verlie away from Troy and ended up dead. Their attitude offended her. They ended up naked and dead in their truck after Verlie told her, "fuck them Cundliff's all to hell."

"Later on, when they were together out at the creek, Troy hurt Verlie's private parts," Olive told the detective. "Then he disappeared. That was no coincidence," she told Mank. "I don't know where he went, but I'm sure Verlie had something to do with it."

Mank thought Olive made sense. He didn't respond, he just let her rattle on, hoping she'd disclose something else he could use.

Then, according to Olive, "Boone Tompkins started getting pushy with her and he ended up falling off a grain bin ladder. The scariest thing," she added, "is Verlie thinks you've gotten too nosey, and I've gotten too friendly with you, and she's used those same words about you."

"What words, Olive?" asked Mank.

Olive was embarrassed to say the words again. Even over the phone she radiated the heat of her embarrassment. But she couldn't be any help in protecting Mank if she held back. At that point she knew she also put herself in harm's way, but didn't care.

"Fuck him all to hell."

Mank agreed they were troubling coincidences. Verlie could be behind Troy's disappearance, but the circumstances surrounding the deaths of the Cundliffs and Boone were too weird to attribute to a fifteen-year-old girl. Still, Mank had seen some strange things over the span of his career, so he didn't reject Olive's concerns out of hand. She was sincere and he wanted to treat her as such. There may be some layers of truth under the veneer of odd coincidences. After reassuring her, Mank asked Olive if he was to look one place to get a handle on Troy's disappearance, where would that be?

"If it were me, I'd check out the creek," said Olive.

"Yes, that place," said Mank

Word got back to Verlie that there were something going on down at Silver Creek. One of the boys in her Geography class had passed by there on his way into school. He asked her if she knew what was going on.

"I don't know what you're talking about," Verlie told him. "Haven't been there in weeks. Since when am I the goddamned expert on Silver Creek?"

The boy told her everyone knew she liked to fish the creek. On the way into school, he saw several vehicles parked along the road near there. At least two sheriff's squad cars and a fire rescue vehicle. He figured she might know something. Verlie shrugged and walked out to find Olive.

"It's that goddamn detective," she mumbled out loud. "Fuck him all to hell."

When she found Olive outside the classroom ready to come in, she pulled her aside and asked her what she knew about the goings on down at Silver Creek. Olive tried to back away from Verlie, but Verlie pressed closer.

"What's your detective friend up to down at the creek, Olive?"

Olive started to sweat. "I don't know. He didn't say anything about it to me."

Verlie glared at Olive and Olive's face reddened and throbbed. She was nervous and it showed.

"Dammit, Olive, don't play dumb with me. I know you too well."

Verlie's insult stung. At that point, Olive was glad she had told Mank her suspicions. Maybe he'd haul Verlie off to jail and she wouldn't have to tolerate her insults and threats.

"You're pissed off at me, Olive?" asked Verlie. "That's tough shit. You turned on me first."

Olive realized Verlie was listening to her thoughts. She tried to back away, but Verlie pressed closer. Olive started sweating more under her arms and around her waist. Verlie had always been sharp-tongued and derisive, but Olive now felt threatened, physically, for the first time in their friendship.

"Don't hurt me, Verlie," she muttered.

"I'm not going to hurt you, Olive, you simple shit. I wanted to know what you told that detective to make him go back down to Silver Creek. But I can see you didn't tell him much. He probably had the idea before you talked to him. But you did tell him to check out the creek again, right?"

"No, I didn't."

"You can't lie to me, Olive, you know that. Now I've got something I want you to do to make up for your betrayal. I want you to go into the room and tell the teacher I got sick. Tell her I puked or got the cramps or something. Tell her I headed home, okay?"

"Okay."

"I'll see you later."

"Okay."

Verlie walked out of the school and hopped on her bike. She pedaled as fast as she could, heading toward the creek. When she drew near the path into the creek from the road, she slowed down. She saw the official vehicles and, for the first time since Troy disappeared, she was nervous about what happened, and her stomach was in knots.

She didn't stop. She pedaled her bike past the well-worn entry to the creek, which was blocked by official vehicles. About twenty-five yards further south was another break in the undergrowth. On occasion, she and Troy followed this alternative path to the creek bank if they wanted to fish another spot. The vegetation was thicker and the bugs even worse and the path more difficult to traverse but following it would allow her to flank the cops and rescue workers.

Once she worked her way through the vegetation and the clouds of mosquitoes, she hunkered down on the creek bank and watched the men. She saw Mank and several other cops. Her first instincts were to curse them all, but there were too many. It would be hard to explain them away. Also, she wanted to let them go so she could see what they were up to. Why were they down at the creek? No one could have known she sunk Troy's belongings in the creek. She didn't even tell

Olive. Was it a lucky guess on the cop's part? Or was it an act of desperation?

The water flowed fast in the creek and whatever might have been in that muddy water should have been swept away weeks ago. The creek fed into a nasty drainage river where it mingled with brown water, sewage and trash. If anything of Troy's drifted as far as the river, it would be gone for good. However, Verlie started to grow nervous again when she saw two of the men come back from the road with diving gear. They had on wetsuits and carried diving masks and scuba tanks.

She berated herself: why did she have to be so goddamned stupid as to sink Troy's stuff in the creek where they fished all the time? Drama? Narrow thinking? She should have dug a hole and buried it on the farm in the sty, or in the woods behind the house. It was a stupid shit thing to do, she told herself. Something Olive might have done.

She sat on her haunches and watched the divers wade into the water and disappear under the surface. She tracked the bubbles rising to the surface of the muddy water as the men moved slowly toward the opposite bank. She saw one of them surface near the dead tree, the tree where the catfish gather and talk, the one where Troy caught the big flathead. The diver went back down. Then he was up again, heading back to the bank where Mank stood. When the diver got to the bank, he raised his arm and showed Mank a feed sack.

"This was snagged on that dead tree," he said. "About five feet down."

Verlie's heart sank. Snagged. "Fuck that old tree all to hell," she whispered.

Mank took the sack and slowly opened it. One piece at a time he took out Troy's clothing and laid it all in the clearing on the bank. He took out the boots. Then the axe head.

The plaid cowboy shirt, stained brown by the muddy creek water, was buttoned all the way up to the collar; the skivvies were grimy as well; there was a belt in loops of the blue jeans buckled with a gaudy western buckle. The boots, long and narrow and filled with fine sediment, were laced and tied, with socks stuffed inside. Verlie saw Mank shake his head but couldn't hear what he said.

"Lucky find, you fat fuck," Verlie mumbled. She wondered how much Olive really knew, what she had told him. She'd deal with Olive later, she thought. If there is a later.

Verlie worked her way back on the path and mounted her bicycle. She figured she'd ride back to school and finish the day, as if nothing had happened. It would give her time to think about her next steps.

Mank looked at his wristwatch. Verlie Martin would still be in school, he reasoned, and it would give him time to go out to the Martin place before she got home. He wanted to talk to Little John about the sack of clothes.

Little John piddled around inside the fence of the hog lot when Mank parked his car. He walked behind the Martin house toward the hog operation, following the stink and swatting at the flies. He toted the burlap sack containing the clothes, the boots and axe head. He hailed Little John.

"Mr. Martin? Can you give me a few minutes?"

Little John walked across the sty, his rubber boots sinking in mud, making a sucking sound with each step. The smell of the place was nauseating. But Mank's satisfaction with the developments of the day kept him focused on the task at hand and he ignored the stench. When Little John got to the fence in front of him, Mank held up the sack and asked, "You recognize this, Mr. Martin?"

Little John squinted at the sack, trying to focus on the faded lettering on the burlap.

"That's an old Master Mix feed sack. My old man fed Master Mix to his hogs when I was a boy. I keep a few of 'em around here. He used to buy feed in those burlap sacks. Now they package it in paper bags. Or I buy in bulk and the mill delivers it; depends."

"You have some of these sacks around here?"

"I got a handful of them I keep in the feed house. They come in handy now and then. Why?"

"Curious."

Mank opened the sack and took out the pieces of clothing, and one-by-one showed them to Little John. "You recognize any of these articles of clothing?"

"Can't say as I do, although that belt buckle in them jeans favors one Troy Cundliff wore. I seen it on him at the Gas Mart."

"Could you say for sure it's Troy's?"

"Not me. Verlie might know."

"What about this?" asked Mank when he held up the axe head.

"Let me see that," said Little John. Mank handed him the hardware across the fence. Little John turned it over and over in his hands. "I believe this is my doorstop I been missing."

"Doorstop?"

"You see it's an axe head," said Little John with a chuckle. "But I kept it in the feed house and used it as a door stop now and then. I've been looking high and low for it."

"I'll see if I can get it back to you when I'm done with it," said Mank.

"Where'd you find all this stuff?" asked Little John.

"In Silver Creek," said Mank. "You have any idea how it could have gotten there?"

"Me? No. But folks dump all sorts of crap in that creek. Heck, when I was a kid, I seen a whole refrigerator bobbing down that creek after a heavy rain."

"Do me a favor, will you, Mr. Martin? Don't mention this to anyone. I don't want any wild rumors starting, okay? Don't even mention it to Verlie until I get a chance to talk to her about it."

Mank said goodbye to Little John and started back towards his car.

"Hey, detective," hollered Little John. "You didn't happen to find that no good Troy Cundliff in that creek, did you?"

"Not yet, Mr. Martin. Not yet."

25.

When Verlie got home from school, she changed her clothes and headed out to the pig sty.

She did some of her best thinking when feeding the pigs. She needed to think. She reasoned Mank would be coming to see her. She'd seen him go through Troy's belongings at the creek. But so what? If Troy wanted to vanish, it wouldn't be that odd for him to have sunk his clothes in the creek. But why? She'd have to think on that awhile.

The axe head was a problem. She could argue Troy took it to make weight to the sack. But when did he steal it? The same time he made the prints behind that feed house. That fit together pretty good. But why was he behind the feed house? Why Little John's axe head? How did he know it was there? That was going to take some figuring.

The pigs snuffled through the troughs as Verlie dumped the feed. She wracked her brain, pouring over the exigencies. She needed to account for everything.

"You pigs got it made; you know?" she asked. "You just eat and shit."

Her story building was a fatiguing exercise. Every time she came up with an angle, some other fact blunted the point. She went inside the feed house to get another bucket of feed. When she came out, Little John stood near the fence.

"That detective was here today."

"What did he want?" asked Verlie.

"He had a sack full of Troy Cundliff's duds. Found them sunk in Silver Creek."

"Really?"

"You know anything about 'em?"

"Why would I?"

"'Cause Big John's old single bit axe head was in the sack."

Verlie didn't respond. Her mind spun round and round. Finally, she said, "He likely stole it."

"How'd he even know it was here?"

Verlie leaned against the fence and sighed. She rubbed her eyes as if to clear them of the fog of stink. She coughed and she stammered:

"I didn't want to ever tell you this, Little John, but Troy was here not long before he left. I was feeding and he snuck up on me in the feed house. He wanted to stick his pecker in me, and I wouldn't let him. I picked up the axe head and told him I'd brain him if he didn't stop and get away from me. He snatched the axe out of my hand and took off. "

Little John was silent for a moment, then he said, "You should have told me sooner, girl."

"You'd a kilt him if I had."

"Surely I would have, child. Surely I would have."

"I figure that's why he took off," said Verlie.

"He isn't as stupid as he looks," said Little John as he put his arm across Verlie's shoulder. "But if he ever comes back to Emery, I'll feed his ass to Old Ott."

26.

Sheriff Billy Phillips sat in his chair, feet on the desk, smoking a cigarette and listening to Detective Sam Mank's briefing on the Troy Cundliff case. Sheriff Phillips didn't want to hear what Mank had to say, but it went with the job. From the first words out of Mank's mouth, the Sheriff recognized that no one would be satisfied with the detective's investigation, particularly Troy's sister Mae Tompkins.

"The creek turned out to be a key to the case," Mank told Phillips. "The divers found that sack full of clothes and boots hung up on a dead cottonwood branch about five feet deep in the water. Weirdest thing I ever saw. Cundliff's outfit was stashed in the bag and looked like it had been packed in there for safe storage. As I told you before, the sack was weighted down with a single bit axe head."

"You think Cundliff tossed the sack in the creek himself?"

"That's the only thing I can figure, Billy."

"Don't make sense. If he was going to take off, why get rid of the clothes?"

"I didn't say it made sense. I said it's the only thing I can figure. Cundliff wanted out of Emery and wanted to leave everything behind."

"Because some girl's daddy was going to kill him?"

"As good a reason as any."

"Little John Martin?"

"As good a suspect as any."

"Look, Sam, this doesn't ring true. Too many holes."

Mank started over, telling the facts in greater detail:

"You know Troy Cundliff had an eye for young girls. I saw his collection of porn in his bedroom myself. It also seems he had an eye for Verlie Sue Martin. I think he groomed her, taking her fishing, spending time with her, you know. Anyway, he knew Verlie's routine. Verlie says he showed up at the Martin's one evening when she was alone in the feed house. He tried to have his way with her. She threatened to hit him with the axe head. Cundliff also knew Little John could be a mean little son-of-a-bitch, so he panicked and took off."

"That's Verlie's story, right?" asked the Sheriff. "What makes you think she's telling the truth?"

"I saw it in her face, Billy. I've been doing this a long time."

"Any corroboration?"

"I followed up with Olive Crowley. She told me Troy tried to have sex with Verlie once before."

"Verlie didn't tell her folks?"

"She figured Little John would kill Troy if he knew. She didn't want her daddy going to jail. But it took care of itself when Troy skipped town."

"I don't know, Sam. This is all too weird. Why didn't he take his truck?"

"If he is in the Army, he didn't need his truck."

Phillips lit another cigarette. "What am I supposed to tell Mae Tompkins?"

"Tell her the facts as we know them. Tell her I can't find Troy and I can't find anyone to blame for his disappearance. She's gonna have to live with it."

"Easy for you to say."

"This is easier: I'm done with this case, Billy. I know it has holes in it, but I don't think I want to know any more about the Cundliffs, or Verlie Martin, or even Olive Crowley."

"Something spook you, Sam?"

"Spooked? Nah. But there are some things in life you're better off not knowing."

27.

The day after Detective Mank confronted Little John, Verlie got to
school early and waited on the front steps for Olive. As Olive clomped
down the bus steps, Verlie shook her head and thought, my God, you are
a homely thing, and she grinned at Olive and waved her over.

"I guess we're done with that goddamned detective friend of yours,"
she said to Olive as Olive sat down next to her on the top step. "I fed
Little John a line of shit about Troy trying to stick his pecker in me out in
the feed house. I told him I figured Troy vamoosed before he got wind
of it and killed him. I do believe my old man swallowed it, hook, line and
sinker, as Troy used to say. Little John called that detective and had him
come out. I explained it all to him, too. He told me he's wrapping up his
investigation. We should be back to normal around here, Olive."

"What's normal, Verlie?"

"Not me, for sure."

"What about Mae?"

"Mae? I think all Mae needs is a good meal and a few pounds on her
bones," she said as she got up to the ringing of the bell.

Verlie turned to Olive on the steps and said, "You know, Olive, I
think I'll have Frances drive me over to the Tompkins's place and take
her a slab of bacon and a half a cured ham. I want to express my
condolences for everything, you know? Mae was the best of those
Cundliffs. She was always good to me. It's the least I can do."

The End

www.ingramcontent.com/pod-product-compliance
Lightning Source LLC
Chambersburg PA
CBHW050350030726
47503CB00008B/2710